Forever Love

ROBERT McGUIRE JR

ISBN: 978-1-953709-25-7 paperback
ISBN: 978-1-953709-26-4 ebook

Printed in the United States of America

In memory of my father and brother,
whom I miss always.

1

I woke up this morning still feeling the jet lag from my flight late last night. I knew better to work a double flight; but Lisa was out sick, and they need a flight attendant to fill in for a round-trip flight leaving for Dallas. It worked out well because it meant that I have the next two days off. I love my job as a flight attendant. Soon, I will have enough airtime to apply for international flights. I know that I will have to move, but it comes with the territory. My apartment is small but has a living room, a small kitchen, a bedroom, and a bathroom. I do not need much since I travel a lot.

One night, as I was sleeping, I had an eerie, almost haunting dream. I was standing on top of what seemed to be clouds, which were really more like a fog. There was nothing but blue sky wherever I looked. A figure seemed to appear not in a physical form but in a transparent one, as if it where a ghost though it wasn't. It seemed to be an angel. The angel looked at me and smiled. He pointed to something that I could not see. He must've noticed that I did not understand what was going on since he beckoned me to follow him. I began walking. We walked for what seemed to be several minutes. I could not see anything but the angel that was my guide and the clouds below my feet. Then the cloud-like mist began to fade, and when it completely dissipated, I noticed that we were standing in a hospital ward. I was transparent to everyone around me. They could not see or hear me, but I could see and hear eve- rything around me. The angel pointed to a room. I walked over to it and tried to push against the door, but my hand went right through the door. I was a little scared at first but decided to walk through it.

I passed through the door and noticed that it was just like any hospital suite, with a bed and someone lying in it. At first, I could not make out who this person was lying in the bed, so I moved around the bed to get a closer look. To my surprise, it was Bryan. This startled me, and before I could make sense of everything, the dream faded. This was the only dream that I had this night. I have not had a dream about Bryan in over two years. *Why is this happening now?*

I was still a little puzzled over the dream but decided to get out of bed. I walked over to the bathroom and cleaned up. I brushed my teeth and turned on the shower. I climbed into the shower and stood there for a few minutes, letting the warm water run down my face and trickle down my whole form. I closed my eyes for just a moment and again saw the vision of Bryan lying in a hospital bed. I stood there shaking for a few moments and decided to fin- ish showering.

I walked out of the bathroom and into the kitchen, still drying my hair. I took the teapot from off the stove and filled it with water. Then I put it back on the stove and turned the stove on to boil some water for a cup of instant coffee.

Holding a cup of hot coffee, I walked into the living room and over to the answering machine. I noticed that it was flashing. It was flashing last night when I arrived home, but I had decided that I was too tired to listen to the messages. I pushed the message button on it. It said that there were three new messages.

I pushed the button again and listened to the first message. It was an insurance agent trying to sell life insurance, so I deleted it. The second message was from Micha telling me to call her as soon as I got in. She was a good friend of mine that I have not seen in awhile. I would call her later to see if she would like to go out tonight or tomorrow night. I would be nice to see her. The third message was from Insuk. She wanted me to call her and it was very important. She said that Bryan was very sick and was in the hospital.

I picked up the phone and proceeded to call Insuk. As the phone rang a few times, I looked over to the clock to see what time it was. It was now 8:12 a.m.

"Hello, who is it?" Insuk answered. "It is Misun," I said.

The phone ringing woke Insuk up. She now cleared her head and said, "Misun, you need to come back to North Carolina as soon as you can. Bryan is very sick, and the doctors say that he is dying."

I dropped the phone; slid to the floor, spilling my cup of coffee everywhere; and cried. When I regained a little self-control, I reached for the phone. Insuk was still listening.

"I will try to be on the next flight to North Carolina, if at all possible. How are the children doing?"

"They are very sad but holding on and praying for their dad to get well. Bryan's older sister is taking care of them for now," answered Insuk.

"Thank you for calling and letting me know. I will be there as soon as I can. Please tell the children that I love them and that I will be there very soon. Take care and good-bye." Misun hung up the phone.

Bryan was my first husband. I left him and our two chil- dren after eleven years of marriage. I destroyed him emotion- ally as well as financially, but he still loved me and forgave me after everything that I did to him and our children. Before and after our divorce, if I had a question or needed something, he was glad to help. Over the last two years, he had always been there for me. It hurt me—and made me feel incessantly guilty—because I was never there for him nor the children.

I sat on the floor for several minutes stunned by the news of Bryan. I began to cry once more. I used the towel that I was drying my hair with to clean up the spilled coffee. I stood up and walked into the bedroom. I picked out some casual clothes from the closet and laid them out on the bed. I walked into the living room, opened the door to the front closet, and took out a small suitcase. It did not take me very long to pack up what I needed for the trip to North Carolina. I finished dressing, walked back out into the living room, picked up the phone, and made reserva- tions for the next flight out to North Carolina.

I made my reservations and was told that my flight was leaving at 12:30 p.m. today on flight number 112760. I looked at the flight number, and it reminded me of something. I just could not remember what—Oh yeah! I remember that this was also Bryan's date of birth. November 27, 1960. *This is all very strange.*

I looked at the clock and noticed that it was now 10:20 a.m. I did not have very much time to finish packing and get to the airport. I ran into the bedroom and looked at my suitcase, which was still on the bed. I had already packed up my clothes now I had to finish packing a few more items needed for the trip. I knew that I would forget something, but I decided that I will have to figure that out later. I also had no time to put on my makeup, so I would have to do this later as well.

I reached over to the dressing table and picked out the jewelry that I was going to wear. I opened the necklace case and noticed that the necklace that Bryan made for me before I left them two years ago was glowing. I reached for it, and as soon as I touched it, a flash of light filled the room. Suddenly, I was struck by a vision. It was of Bryan holding his book. Then just like that, the vision was gone. I remembered that he wrote a book once. The story was similar to that of our life together, but it was more focused on the necklace—the very necklace that he gave to me.

I held the necklace around my neck, and for whatever reason, the necklace always seemed to fill me with a sense of inner peace. Bryan once told me that whenever I needed help or when I felt sad, if I wear the necklace, it would bring me good luck. I have often worn the necklace; and on those occasions when I needed help or felt sad, the necklace felt warm, and (like Bryan said) my problems seemed to go away.

I picked up my suitcase and started for the door. I took one last look at my apartment to make sure that I did not leave anything on. Satisfied with the hasty inspection, I opened the door and headed out to my car. I placed the suitcase in the trunk, got into the car, and drove to the airport. On the way, I thought of the events of this morning.

I kept thinking how this was all connected, and I always came up with the same conclusion: everything had to do with this necklace and Bryan's book. I never read his book, but I had so many questions. And somehow, I just knew that I may find some of the answers in the book. Bryan never said what he meant and always left questions unanswered. *I will need to make one more stop, but that will have to wait until I get to North Carolina.*

2

I opened my eyes from a very restless sleep and looked out into the room. Everything was still white and smelled of disinfectant. I lay here in a hospital bed, which has been my home for the last two days now. The only things that were cheerful in this room were the flowers, the stuffed animals that my friends and family had brought as gifts for me, and the window that gave me a view of the sunset.

I did worry about Rachel and Junior. My sister, Anna, and her husband, David, flew in the day before. They were going to stay at my house and watch over the kids while I was in the hospital.

My time in this world had run short, and I am the one who caused it. I did not regret what I had done. This was the way it had to be. It was the *only* way. I was not sure exactly how much time I had left, but I knew that it had to be just a day or two. That's all. The doctors had run so many different tests on me but did not find anything wrong with me. They still wanted to find out why this was happening to me. I give them credit for the fact that they had to jus- tify everything with science. I'd hate to tell them that some things just cannot be justified that way.

I started to write down the events over the last two years before I entered the hospital, and I was glad that I had finished. It had been very tiring and difficult at times. My health and strength had been worsening quite rapidly. These notes will explain everything—even my secret.

I did not notice that while I was deep in thought, Anna and the kids entered the room. I looked over at Rachel and Junior and noticed that they were waiting for me to say something. It hurt me to see them. I just could not help feeling so sorry for them. I had brought this pain upon them, who were the innocent party in all of this. They were going to have to really feel the pain of their father leaving them. And it was tearing me apart.

I so much wanted to tell them what I had done, but I could not break the oath that sealed my fate. I knew that Anna and David would take care of them and raise them as if they were their own. After all, I did not make them Rachel and Junior's legal guardians in my will for nothing.

I decided that I had better say something before they started getting worried. I looked at Rachel and Junior, trying very hard to hold back the tears that started to form in my eyes. With half a smile, the only thing that I could say was "I love you." Rachel and Junior ran over and climbed onto the bed to be close to me. They looked up at me with their eyes ready to burst with tears and said, "I love you too."

I could not help myself this time. I cried. We held each other and let it all out. For the first time, I felt sorrow and guilt. All I could do was hold them, not wanting to let them go.

After a few minutes, I looked across the room and saw Anna and David crying too. I talked with Rachel and Junior for a little while, telling them to be good and to listen to their aunt and uncle. They nodded because they could not bring themselves to say anything. I asked them if I could speak with Aunt Anna and Uncle David for a few minutes. They just nodded.

A nurse who just stepped into the room said that she was taking the children to the waiting room until I called for them. She must have been just outside the door. I thanked her and kissed the kids and sent them off on their way. I felt all alone as they walked out of my room. I hoped that someday, they will be able to forgive me.

Anna and David walked over to me and held my hand. I had to fight back the tears once again so that I could speak to them. Anna was the only one in the family with whom I could talk about anything. She was the oldest daughter, and I was the oldest son. We carried that in common while growing up. I cannot explain it more aptly than that we were *the same but different.*

She'd always been my best friend, and I loved her very much. She always called me her little brother, and on occasions, she called me Bryan. I so much wanted to tell her my story, but I just could not. This will have to be my secret, which will have to leave with me. She will read about it after I am gone. I noticed that she kept trying to smile, but it was clearly very hard for her. She was fighting back the tears as well.

David, who stood there wearing a half-smile and swollen eyes, could not speak either. I went straight to my point: I asked them to take good care of Rachel and Junior. I told them that I loved them and that I was sorry for everything. I said that I had arranged for them and that within my safe at home there are a few documents that will need address- ing when the time comes.

"Junior will open the safe for you. He knows how. The folder that you will need is labeled Will."

Anna bent over, kissed Bryan, and said, "I love you too, Little Brother."

David, still looking sad and holding back his tears, said, "The kids will be fine. Is there anything else that I can do for you?"

Bryan smiled and said, "Never change."

Bryan looked over at Anna and asked her, "Could you find the nurse and bring the kids back into the room for me?"

Anna did not reply; she just nodded her head and left the room.

After a few minutes, the kids reentered the room. Rachel and Junior both ran over to the bed and climbed on it to be close to me. They both hugged me, and for the first time, Junior spoke.

Junior, holding back his tears, said, "Will I always remember you, Daddy?"

"I will always be in your heart and memories. I will never leave those places within you. Just think of me when you need me, and your memories of me will be with you," answered Bryan.

Junior, looking a little unsure, asked, "What if need you tomorrow?"

Bryan smiled and said, "I will be here tomorrow and the rest of your life, not as you see me now but as you see me within your heart."

Junior smiled and gave Bryan a kiss. Then he said, "I love you, Dada."

Rachel's going to be the one that I'm going to have the hardest time with. She was trying so hard to be strong and grown up. She was indeed my sweetheart. Without her, I do not know how we could have lasted so long. She was the woman of the house since her mother left.

She took care of Junior and me when we were sick. She helped me straighten up and clean the house when I was tired. I taught her how to cook and sew clothes. She taught me how to understand her needs being a pre-teen. She was only twelve years old but seemed to be going on eighteen. She was my strength and hope. I depended on her too much. And she always did as I asked without question.

She asked me if I needed anything. She was playing her role as mom now, and I thought of how precious she really was. I feared for her because she was so innocent and could be so easily hurt. I knew that David and Anna will guide her and teach her to be strong. I told Rachel that the only thing that I needed right now was a big hug and a kiss. She gave me a squashy hug and a big kiss.

Upon seeing this, Junior did not want to be outdone, so he joined in with another squashy hug and a big kiss. I told them that I was going to miss them and that I will see them tomorrow. They both kissed me one more time and hopped off the bed saying, "See you tomorrow, Daddy," as they walked out of the room to meet up with Anna and David.

Misun and I were truly blessed with two beautiful and caring children. I prayed every night, thanking God for our beautiful children.

After they had left the room, I began to cry softly to myself. I somehow felt that this was the last night that we would have together. It was almost over now, yet there was still something missing.

The nurse entered the room and brought me something to eat. She was a very kind nurse and sometimes treated me as if I were a child. I would just smile and do as she asked.

She asked me, "Is there anything else you need?" I told her, "I need a cigarette."

She just smiled and said, "I don't think that you need a cigarette. Those things will kill you. You do need to eat, however."

I had not smoked a cigarette in over two years. It was a little joke between us. I'd finish eating what I could. Then she'd come back into the room and scold me for not finishing my dinner. I'd tell her maybe tomorrow.

As she walked out of the room, I looked out the window and up at the night sky. I looked at the stars and the moon. I loved looking at the stars and the moon with the kids. I used to think that a star was a person's soul that had gone to heaven. From there, they could look down upon the earth and still see their loved ones. A falling star, on the other hand, was a soul coming back to earth for a visit. I wondered if I was going to be one of those stars someday.

3

I thought that I would never make to the airport on time. Traffic was just terrible. I parked the car and opened the trunk to pullout the suitcase. I just happened to look at my watch. I noticed that it was now 11:50. I really did not have time to waste. I hurried to the first class check- in counter. My ticket was prepaid and so all I had to do was get my seat assignment and have my suitcase checked in. Luckily, there was no one at waiting at the counter so it only took me five minutes to check in. The woman at the counter said that the plane was already boarding and I needed to hurry.

I picked up my seat assignment and headed to the boarding gate. I was the last passenger to board the plane. As soon as I boarded the plane, they closed the doors behind me. I moved to my seat. It was only going to be a two-hour flight.

I settled into my seat and tried to relax. For the first time, I touched the necklace, and it did not flash me with another vision except that I felt warm and seemed to relax me for the time being. I still felt the sense of urgency but there was no way I was going to get there any faster.

I seemed to dose off…

· · · · · · ●●●●●●●●●●●● · · · ·

Bryan stationed in Korea for the last five months and just extended for another year; he took leave and flew back to North Carolina on leave to pick up the kids and me to travel back to Korea with him. I had many problems with finances during this time. I felt very bad for Bryan because he was living on fifty dollars a month. The army was feeding him and providing him a place to live but any other expenses that he had would come out of that fifty dollars. We agreed the best thing to do was to rent out the house and that everyone would go back with him. I had family there and I would be closer to Bryan and my family.

The whole eighteen months in Korea was a complete disaster. We seemed to have not fewer problems but more. Bryan's work kept him away from the house most of the time and the army did not pay for the children's school because we where on a non-command sponsored tour in army terms that meant you are on your own. Money was very tight and I had to find work. I started working in a bank on post but it did not pay enough. Therefore, I went to work at a club downtown. Bryan objected but he did not peruse the matter.

Bryan was able to talk to his commander and was able to come home every night that he was not in the field or staff duty. That helped, so he watched the kids while I went to work.

Bryan walked the children to school every morning and I would pick them up in the afternoon. Depending on when I came home from work, I would forget sometime, they would walk home by themselves, the streets where safe, and their school was not far, so I thought that that would be okay. Bryan would get very upset at me when I forgot to pick them up. He then talked to one of the teach- ers and arranged for them to bring them home.

Between Bryan's work, my family problem and finical problems then a flood during the monsoon season that took away everything that we owned was too much for me, I just could not take it any more. I was staying later after work and started to drink. On weekends when Bryan was home, I went out with my friends sometimes I would not return home until the next day. My world was crashing and I did not care.

The army scheduled Bryan to leave for school before reassigned to North Carolina. He tried to extend for another year. He so wanted to try to get our life back in order but the army denied the request and ordered him to school. I will never forget the day he left. For the first time he felt helpless and wished that, he could do something else. We spent our last night together at a friend's house. The next morning we went to the airport. I kissed him good-bye and he boarded the plane.

After Bryan left, my mother stayed with the children and me so I could go to work. She did not approve of me working at a nightclub and would always remind me of it every day. I did not need to hear this not now. I would sometimes be gone two days, at times just so that I did not have to listen to my mother. I was still drinking and gambling with my friends. Bryan would call every three days to see how we where doing but I always would give him the same response telling him that we where all fine and that the kids loved him and missed him. I did not want Bryan to know about my problems because school was very important for him right now and he needed to finish.

Bryan's school lasted for two months, I finally told him that we where having more money problems and He said that he would sort them out when we all get back to North Carolina. This was three days before his graduation.

He called me again the day before his graduation and told me that he is the distinguished honor graduate of his class. He was very happy and could not wait to see all of use very soon in California. I was going to meet Bryan in California with the kids. We would stay in California for a few days and be with his family. We were going to drive back to North Carolina and stop off in Texas to visit his sister on the way. Bryan and the kids loved road trips but I did not care to travel by car. It was then that I told him that we needed to separate and I asked him if he would take care of the kids. There was a pause of silence; he said that he could take care of the children. I know that I just crushed him and he was only thinking of the kids. I just wanted out and to be left alone.

A few days later, I took the kids to the airport. It was a very sad for all of us. Bryan had to call the airport and arranged for them to fly to California without a parent. They would have an appointed guardian on the plane to attend their needs while they traveled to California. Bryan would have to sign for them before they would release the children to him. I kissed the children and watched them board the plane. I felt so sorry for them. Rachel was eight years old and Junior was only four. I cried to myself and left the airport.

After five months alone in Korea, I met Kevin. Kevin would stay after the club closed and talk to me. We talked about many different things and he would walk me home. He made me feel so comfortable and for a change, I was not alone anymore. We were together for a few months when one night after the club closed he took me home, hugged, and kissed me. I felt very warm and at peace. I gave myself to him that night and told him that I loved him. He told me that he loved me too. We talked about getting married after the divorce with Bryan finalized. I still had nightmares of when I placed the children on the plane. It hurt me so bad that I wanted to die. Kevin was the only one that helped me through this time and stopped me from taking my own life at one point.

Bryan and I had been divorced for a few months when I really wanted to see the children in North Carolina; Kevin had to leave on a mission. He asked me if I was going to be okay and I told him that I would be fine. He gave me his cell phone number and e-mail address so we could keep in touch. We kissed each other and he left for his mission. He would be gone for a few weeks. I decided to fly to Colorado and link up with my friend Miyon. She was divorced and her two children were with her ex-husband. We had a lot in common.

I meet Miyon in Colorado and we talked about everything. I had not seen her in two years and we had much to say to each other. I told her about Kevin and she was shocked to hear this. She then asked about Bryan and the children. I told her that I felt sorry for Bryan and the chil- dren but I have a new life now and that I just wanted to see the kids.

Miyon was divorced for two years and had two children. We drank and cried together because we missed our children. That night we decided to call our ex-husbands to talk to the children. She called first. She cried when se talked to the children and then hung up the phone. It was now my turn. I picked up the phone and started to dial the number. I have not had a conversation with Bryan and the children in over the last fourteen months except when I called him and asked for a divorce. When I asked for the divorce six months ago, he cried. I knew that Bryan still love me and wished that I would go to him. I did not want his love nor did I want to be with him because I now have Kevin and I just wanted to see the children.

The phone rang three times before Bryan answered it. "Hello" he said.

Misun feeling very nervous replied, "It is me. Misun." "It has been awhile since you called. Is everything okay?" Bryan asked.

"Everything is fine," I replied. I was wondering if I could come out to North Carolina to see Rachel and Junior. I am here in Colorado with Miyon and she is going to see her children in Charlotte." Misun said feeling a little skeptical. Bryan was now feeling very excited answered, "Yes, when will you be coming?"

Felling no longer nervous and now very excited about going to see her children Misun said, "We will be leaving as early as tomorrow and it will take us a couple of days to drive there. Can you meet me in Charlotte? If you pick me up, I will be able to stay a few days and visit with the kids if that was all right."

"That would be fine. I will tell the kids that you will be here in a few days. We have missed you." Bryan said.

Feeling a little bit guilty knowing that Bryan has been waiting for over fourteen months to see her, she was now on my way to see her children and Bryan was something that she was going to have to deal with when she arrived said, " I will call you when we are close. I know it is late there and you need to sleep but thank you for letting me come."

"It is all right, it was worth a few minutes sleep to hear your voice again and to hear the great news that you are coming to see us. I will be waiting to hear from you and be careful on your trip." Bryan said.

With all of this said, they both shared there good-byes and place the phones back on the receivers.

Misun looked at Miyon and said, "Everything is okay with Bryan. We need to pack and get some sleep."

They hugged each other and begun packing their suit-cases and went to sleep.

It felt as if I only slept a few minutes before Miyon shook me telling me to get up. I knew it was almost time to leave. I got out of bed, walked into the bathroom, washed the sleep out of my eyes, and took a shower. By the time, I finished dressing Miyon had already packed the car. I now that she was very excited to go see her children. I finished gathering a few miscellaneous items and we decided that we would share the driving time. She was going to take the first leg of the drive until she got tired. With that, we looked at each other, got into the car, and headed to North Carolina.

I ended up driving most of the way to North Carolina while Miyon slept. She forgot to tell me that she gets carsick from time to time. That was fine with me for when I was getting too tired we stopped off at a hotel and slept. The trip took us two days. I called Bryan from Knoxville Tennessee and told him that we should be in Charlotte in about three hours. He told me that he had just returned home from work and was going to take a shower, pack up the truck with Rachel and Junior will arrive in Charlotte in about three hours. I gave him Miyon's cell phone number and he said that he would call when he was close. I was in Ashville when he called. He said that he was already in Charlotte. I told him that I had a hard time driving through the mountains and if we could meet somewhere in between. He looked at his map and said that the next place would be Shelby. This was now our new destination.

It took an hour and a half to arrive in Shelby. Bryan called again stating that he was in a McDonalds parking lot right of the interstate next to the mall it was the only one in Shelby, He had arrived thirty minutes prior. I was getting very tired and I did not pay attention to the signs and took the business route into Shelby. Bryan called again and asked me what the name of the closest intersection is where I was. I told him and he directed me to his location. After twenty minutes, we finally arrived in the parking lot of McDonalds. Bryan's truck was nowhere in the parking lot. I stopped the car. The next thing that I knew he was driving into the parking lot. I guess that he went to get some more change for the phone.

As I watched his truck pull into the parking lot, I began to feel very nervous. I really did not know what to expect. I had not seen any of them in over fourteen months now. Bryan stopped the truck in front of the car and Rachel was the first one to get out. She ran over to me. I got out f the car. We hugged each other and began to cry. I told her how much I missed and loved her. She told me that she loved and missed me so so so muche. I asked Bryan where is Junior? Bryan said that he was sleeping in the truck. Bryan walked over to me, hugged me and kissed me on the cheek. I thought that I was strong but when he kissed me, I began to melt in his arms. My lips met his and we kissed.

We offloaded Miyon's car with my things and placed them in the truck. When we opened the truck door, Junior woke up. To his surprise, I was standing there. I began to cry once more. I hugged him and kissed him. He told me that he missed me.

Miyon walked over to the truck and told us that she was going to spend the night here in town before leaving to Charlotte to see her children. I was going to stay with Bryan and the kids for the next few days. We said our good- byes and she got into her car and drove off. I know that it was very late and Bryan had a long drive before we arrived at his house. The time was now 12:05 a.m. It was going to take us four to five hours until we would arrive there. I felt sorry for Bryan. Bryan would not be able to sleep before he had to go into work. He still had a long way to drive. He did not care about the loss of sleep or the fact that he was tired, he was happy now and it was all worth it. I knew this about Bryan.

Bryan and I talked the whole way back. I was very surprised by what he had to tell me. He told me of his struggles over the last fourteen months and that every thing was working out fine now. He also told me how Rachel and Junior have grown up during that time. I felt very sorry for Bryan, he had suffered so much and I was the one that had done all of this to him. He told me that at first he was very mad at me for all of this but forgave me many months ago. He could never stay mad to long. I did not understand how he could forgive me for all of the things that I have done and yet he still loves me.

We arrived at his house at 4:30 a.m. I guess he was in a hurry to get home. I opened the front door to the house and walked in. Bryan had to carry Junior in he was still sleeping. I turned on the lights and saw the house for the first time in years. It was the same old house and was set up exactly the same way as we left it. Bryan walked into the house carrying Junior and placed him into his bed. He walked over to Rachel, kissed her, and told her that she needed to kiss her mom and go to bed as well. He also told her that they where not going to school today and they would spend time with their mom. She was very excited, ran over to me, hugged, and kissed me then she was off to her room.

I was very tired and sat down on the couch in the living room. He still had the same old furniture and it has the same arrangement as the day we left. The only difference in the house was that of the family picture hanging over the fireplace. I felt very much like I was at home. This feeling hurt me. I wanted to cry but held back my tears.

Bryan broke my train of thought for a moment, saying that I should go clean up and get some sleep because when the kids wake up, there was going to be no time for sleeping. I agreed with him and told him that I was going to take a shower. I also asked if he could bring my suitcase into the room for me. He nodded his head and walked out to the truck.

After a few minutes, he walked back into the house, placed my suitcase on the bed, and asked me if I needed anything else. I told him that would be all. I got up from the couch, walked into the bedroom, and noticed the comforter on the bed. I had sent that to him while I was still in Korea. The room was still decorated just as before with that one exception.

I told him that I would sleep on the couch. He looked at me and said that if anyone was going to sleep on the couch, it was going to be him. I told him that he did not have to give up anything for me. He said that it would be fine and that it will all work out. I did not want to upset him. Instead, I asked him how he was feeling. He said that he was tired and that he was going to finish a few things and take a shower before heading off to work.

I finished my shower and was now ready for bed. I slipped into my nightshirt and walked into the bedroom. Bryan walked into the bedroom and pulled the covered back from the bed as if inviting me to lie beside him. I crawled into bed, and he pulled the covers over me. The bed felt so comfortable and warm. I knew that it would not take me long until I start to feel sleepy. Bryan sacrificed his sleep to drive all the way to pick me up.

Bryan kissed me and thanked me for coming. Then he walked into the bathroom to take a shower. I was already half-asleep when he walked out of the bathroom. He walked over to me and kissed me on the forehead. He always kissed me like that before he left for work. I did not even remember the door closing as he left for work.

······•·······

It was now 10:00 a.m., and I found Rachel and Junior lying next to me. In that moment, I felt at home. It all seemed as though everything was just a nightmare that I was now waking up from. I smiled, reached over, and kissed them. I lay there wondering, *Is this really a dream? Because if it is, I don't want to wake up.*

They stirred and opened their eyes. I met their gaze with a big smile. They then crawled over to me, kissed me, hugged me, and told me that they missed me. I knew then that this was not a dream and began to cry.

Bryan had been their mother and father the whole time I was gone, and he had taken very good care of them. He instilled my memory into the kids with all the pictures and keeping the house just as it had been kept before. I think that the pictures were all he had left. Those and the belief that I would return someday.

We all decided to get out of bed, and the first thing that they did was to walk into the bathroom and wash off the sleep from their eyes and brush their teeth. This was the first time that I noticed how much they had grown up. They came out of the bathroom and climbed back onto the bed. They said that I could sleep some more and that they would watch some TV until I decided to get up. I lay there for a few minutes and began to cry by myself. I cried because I missed Rachel and Junior so much. *How could I have done this to them?*

They forgave me without question and they still loved me. I felt so ashamed. I laid there in our house no not our house but Bryan's house. They loved me and forgave me. I never felt so selfish until now. I cried for a few minutes more then decided to get out of bed.

I got out of bed, walked into the bathroom, washed my face, and brushed my teeth. I was dressed and started to put on some makeup when Junior walked into the bath- room. He said that he was hungry and asked me if I could make him some scrambled eggs with ketchup. He said that he loved them. I stopped what I was doing and smiled at Junior and walked out of the bathroom holding Junior's hand as we walked into the kitchen.

The kitchen was the same as everything in the house. I opened the cabinets and pulled out a pan to cook Junior's eggs. I went over to the refrigerator and took out every- thing that I needed. I noticed that Bryan kept the refrig- erator well stocked. I yelled over to Rachel and asked her what she wanted for breakfast. She said that she had already had eaten something for breakfast. I asked her what she had eaten. She said that she ate a sausage, egg biscuit from the freezer. I opened the freezer, looked at the box, and pulled one out. I asked Rachel how to cook it. She told me to place it into the microwave for two minutes.

I asked Rachel when you got a microwave. She said that Aunt Anna gave it to us for Christmas. I was not very hun- gry right now but this just may hit the spot and anyway the kids where more important and it was my job to take care of them first.

As I began cooking for Junior, I felt a little strange cooking for them. Has it been so long? Do they still like the same foods? I have somehow forgotten what they like. I will have to ask them later.

I finished cooking for Junior and placed his plate on the table. I sat down with him and we ate together. After he was finished, he walked his plate over to the sink and placed it into the sink. He has grown up so much he was just a baby when I placed them on that plane. He came over to me, kissed me, thanked me for the breakfast, ran into the bedroom, jumped on the bed, and began to watch TV with Rachel.

I made myself a cup of coffee and decided to take a tour around the house. I had noticed that Bryan hung many certificates of Rachel and Junior I know that he is a very proud father. As I read each certificate, Rachel came out of the room and said that Daddy was very proud of her and Junior, so he places them on the wall. She asked me if I was proud of her as well. I felt like a knife had just stabbed me in the back. I wish that I could have been there for her in her special moment. I looked down at her and told her that I was very proud and that I will always be proud of her and Junior.

The house was full of memories and they where all staring at me haunting me with those memories. I felt so small in this house but I could not stop feeling that I belonged here. I walked into the kid's rooms. I noticed that in each room Bryan had provided everything that they would need from a TV to a computer. Videotapes and books filled the shelves while toys and games filled there toy chests. Each room had many different pictures, their favorite posters and many family pictures. Every room had at least two or three pictures of me. My presence was still here and alive in this house. I think that Bryan did not want the kids to forget me so he placed pictures everywhere.

I walked back out into the living room and into Bryan's bedroom, where the kids were watching TV. I walked to the closet and opened the door. I noticed that Bryan had arranged the closet to suit his needs. He had placed Rachel and Junior's clothes on one side and his on the other. I looked down and saw that his pairs of shoes were placed neatly next to each other, and next to them were mine. I walked back out of the closet and sat down on the bed next to Rachel and Junior. I felt very comfortable, and we all watched TV together.

Much of the rest of the day was spent playing with Rachel and Junior. We jumped on the trampoline and played video games. We also talked about what they'd been doing for the last few months.

Bryan returned at around 5:30 p.m. He walked through the door and looked very tired but still seemed very happy. This was the first time that I noticed that he had lost a lot of weight since I last saw him in Korea. I knew that he worked very hard and his needs were always last.

He walked over and kissed me. Then he asked me how my day with Rachel and Junior went. I said that we spent our day having fun and playing games. I told him of my observation that I was still alive in this house. There were pictures of me and the kids everywhere. I felt very comfortable and thanked him for this. He looked at me very seriously for a moment and said that I could stay if I wanted and that no matter what I decided to do, they were lucky to see me once again. In that moment, I walked over to him, kissed him, and thanked him for everything.

Bryan then said that he was going to take a shower and that we all were going out for dinner. Rachel and Junior asked if we could go out to the Chinese restaurant. Bryan consented. He also asked me if I could make him a cup of coffee, and I said that it would be ready by the time he finished his shower.

Moments later, Bryan walked out of the bathroom and sat down at the dining table. I walked over to him and placed his coffee in front of him. He smiled and thanked me.

He was very quiet as he finished drinking his coffee. Rachel and Junior said that they were all ready to go out to eat. They put on their socks and shoes and seemed to be waiting for us to move. Bryan looked over at the kids and said, "I guess we are all ready." Everyone was ready, except me. I asked everyone to give me five minutes to put on some makeup and change clothes. They all agreed to give me a few minutes to get ready.

They waited for about ten minutes, and then we were all ready to go to dinner. We walked out of the house, got into the truck, and headed to the restaurant. It was a short drive, and I placed my hand on Bryan's as he drove. He smiled.

· · · · · · · · ● · · · · · · · · · ·

The restaurant was a Chinese buffet. All the food looked and smelled delicious. We all sat down and almost imme- diately began eating. When we finished eating, we got back into the truck and drove back home. We all decided to watch TV together until it was time for the kids to go to bed. When it was time for the kids to do so, Bryan and I walked them into their rooms, tucked them in, hugged them, kissed them, and said good night. They both gave us a big hug and kiss and told us that they were very happy and that they had a great day.

We walked back into the living room, and Bryan said that he was very tired and needed to go to sleep. I told Bryan that he could sleep in the bed as I was still going to stay up and watch some TV. He did not complain. He hugged and kissed me before saying good night. He walked into the bedroom, changed his clothes, and crawled into bed. I walked over to the TV and turned it off. I decided that I would go to Bryan. I walked into the bedroom, changed my clothes, and crawled into bed.

I lay there for a moment, not knowing what to do. Bryan made the first move. He reached over to me, kissed me, and thanked me for coming. I drew closer to him and kissed him back. It was then when I decided to give myself to him.

•••••••••●••••••••••

We talked for a few minutes afterward. We both talked so much that I had to stop him from saying anything more. I knew that he was very tired and that he needed his sleep. He smiled and said, "We will talk later." He did add how much he had missed me and loved me. I told him that I missed him too. He smiled again, closed his eyes, and finally fell asleep.

For that moment, I felt very happy. As I lay there, I asked myself, *How could I play with someone's emotions like this? Could I really come home?*

•••••••••●••••••••••

The next morning, Bryan woke up and went into the kitchen. He made two cups of coffee and brought one for me in the bedroom. He sat the cup on the nightstand and sat on the bed next to me. He kissed me on the forehead as he had done so many times before. He then used his finger to trace the outline of my face and touched my hair. I opened my eyes, saw him standing over me, and smiled.

He said, "Good morning, honey. I made you a cup of coffee." I thanked him and asked him what time it was. He told me that it was 7:00 a.m. I told him that it was too early and that he needed to come back to bed. He said that the kids were going to wake up in the next thirty minutes and that they were going to be hungry. I asked him if I could sleep for another hour, and he said that it would be fine. He kissed me and said that he would make sure that the kids did not bother me for at least another hour. He got up from the bed and walked out to the living room, closing the door after him.

For the next few days, we lived a family life, and we all were very happy. I was lost in this new world (or was it the old one?). I did not care about the rest of the world. For now, our world was just perfect.

We all went shopping for groceries and stuff for the kids. Bryan took me to an oriental market so that I could buy some things that I needed for dishes I wanted to cook. I really wanted to cook for Bryan and the kids.

I asked the kids if they still liked Korean food. They said that they still liked Korean food and that their dad cooks it for them almost all the time. I looked over at Bryan and asked him when he learned how to cook Korean food. He just smiled at me. He said that he watched me and my mother cook so many times and enjoyed it so much that he had to try it. He said that at first, it was okay but that he got better every time he cooked. I made Bryan and the kids a deal: I would cook tonight, and Bryan would cook tomorrow. The kids were excited.

We all went home, and I immediately started cooking. I did not let Bryan into the kitchen. (He was very curious about what I was cooking.) I knew that he loved *chap- chae.* Well, he loved the way I made it. I made it with fried fish and some small side dishes. I had Rachel and Junior fix the table while I brought the food. We all sat at the table eating.

Everyone enjoyed the meal. Bryan said that was perfect. He was happy that he was able to eat chapchae again. He said, "Not every place around here knows to make good chapchae." That made me happier to make it for him. Not only that, the kids loved it too!

After we all finished dinner, Bryan and I went into the kitchen and washed the dishes. He was supposed to dry, and I was to wash. Well, it turned out that there was more water on the floor than in the sink. Bryan got a little carried away with the drying towel; he hit me with it a few times. I wanted to return the favor, so I splashed him with the dishwater.

One thing led to another, and we both ended up taking a bath by the sink. The kids just laughed at us.

We cleaned up the kitchen and put away the dishes. We told the kids to watch TV while we went to clean up. Bryan and I went into the bedroom, and let me just say that clean- ing up took a little longer than we thought. The kids were half-asleep when we finally left the bedroom. We put the kids to bed and watched TV together for a while before heading to bed ourselves.

· · · · · · · ● · · · · · · · · ·

It was Bryan's turn to cook today. He said that he was going to make one of the kids' favorite dishes. He spent part of the afternoon preparing his meal. He would not let me into the kitchen this time. He lit up the barbeque and cooked the meat. He had made all of the side dishes earlier. I asked the kids what Bryan was making. They all said that it was very good.

The kids helped set the table while Bryan brought out the food. The main course was *bulgogi* with rice. He made a mashed potato salad with crabmeat and a side dish made with little fish. It smelled very good. We all sat down to eat. The kids could not wait to eat the bulgogi. Bryan cut it up for them and placed it on their plates. I decided to try the bulgogi. It melted in my mouth. The meat was so tender and had a sweet taste to it. It was truly enjoyable. The rest of the meal was just as delicious.

When we finished eating, I told Bryan that he could cook for me any time. The food was great. He just smiled and said it was his pleasure to be able to cook for me. We both washed dishes together without incidents. We all watched TV together. It was now time to put the kids to bed. They already were sleepy. They washed their face and hands, brushed their teeth and got ready for bed. Bryan and I both kissed them and left their rooms. Bryan was tired and said that he was going to bed. I kissed him and thanked him for such a good meal. He smiled and said," Anytime." I received a call late that night and it was Miyon. She asked me about my visit with the children and wondered if I was having any problems with Bryan. I told her that I was having a lovely time and we all where very happy. She said that was very good and wanted to know if I was still going to marry Kevin. I had forgotten about Kevin.

How could I have done this? I was in love with Kevin or I think I am or am I still in love with a memory of Bryan and the kids. Now I am confused. I thought that I would be able to handle this. I was so happy living in this dream where everything was just as it was before. There were no problems in this world except mine. If I stay here, I know that I will never be able to leave. It is so easy to get lost in a dream. I have to get away before it is too late.

I told Miyon that I would be ready to go when she arrived. I asked her when she was heading out to pick me up. She asked me if I was in an adventurous mood. I did not know what to think by this question but I wanted to know what she was thinking. I asked her what she had in mind. She said that there may be a business proposition in Virginia and wanted to know if I want to go with her to check it out. I said that I was up to it and getting away would help me sort things. She said that she would be there tomorrow morning and we both could tell each other about our visits. We hung up the phones and I had to tell Bryan and the kids that I would be leaving.

I walked into the bedroom where Bryan was sleeping. I did not want to wake him but I had no choice. I called to Bryan and he began to stir. Bryan looked up at me and asked me if everything was okay. I told him that I was going with Miyon tomorrow to look into a business proposition in Virginia. He smiled and got up from the bed, and asked, if there was anything that he could help me. Bryan was good at hiding his feeling. I know that he was hurt but still was willing to offer any support to me.

I spent the rest of the night packing and helped Bryan put the kids to bed once more. Bryan had not said anything since I told him. I know that he hurting too. He said that he was going to bed, that I should stay up to much longer, and that I needed my sleep as well. He kissed and hugged me before going off to bed. Bryan kissed me; it was as if he was kissing me for the last time. It was a very caring and compassionate kiss like one would give to someone going on a long journey. I felt as though I have hurt him once again.

I finished packing, walked into the bedroom, and crawled into bed. Bryan was asleep but I so wanted to wake him. I wanted to tell him everything, but I could not. I could only think of going with Miyon and trying to sort everything out.

· · · · · · · ● · · · · · · · · ·

Early the next morning, Miyon showed up, and Bryan helped in packing my things in her car. I had not really slept very well. I was up before everyone else. I walked through the house wanting to look at it once more before I left. We all walked outside and over to Miyon's car. I looked over at Rachel and Junior. They looked up at me with swelling eyes. They both said, "Mommy, are you going away again?" at the same time. This crushed me.

I could not help it. I bent down, hugged them, and kissed them. I told them that I have to go away and take care of a few things. They began crying as much as I was. I could not help feeling guilty that I have to leave them once again. I told them that it will not be for very long and that I will be back to see them again. They made me promise.

We cried and held each other, and I asked them to take care of their daddy and to be good. They just nodded their heads and went into the house. This was not going to be easy, but it was time to say good-bye to Bryan. I could not think of any words to say. He walked over to me and placed a finger on my lips. He said for me to take care of myself and that if I needed anything, he would always be there for me. He then kissed me and hugged me. My eyes began to fill once more with tears, but I could not show them to him. I just turned to the car and got in. Bryan closed the door, waved to me, turned, and went back into the house.

······●······

I woke up when the wheels of the plane touched the ground. I was dreaming of events that happened over two years ago. *Are the events that are happening triggering my memories?* I am unsure of what is happening to me, but I have no time to waste to try to think them through.

4

I looked out the window of my hospital room. It was early morning. I knew that by the way the sun had just started to peek up above the horizon. I love to be able to see the sunrise and enjoy it warmth as it rays reach out across the land touching everything bringing life for a new day.

I had dreamt of the first time that I met Misun.

· · · · · · · ●● ● ●● · · · · · · · ·

It was the middle of September in 1988, I was in South Korea, and I just finished my extension for another year. I have not found what I was looking for but I knew that this was where I was going to find it. For the first ten months while stationed here in Korea, I spent most of my time was spent in the field on maneuvers or down town drinking and sleeping with numerous women. This was not the kind of life that I wanted I was the life of a single man with no ties to anyone or anything. I had spent many of nights wondering down these many streets of TDC looking for something or

46

someone. I did not know what I was looking for but I am sure it will present itself in time. There was a reason I was here and it was not just because the army said I had to be here, but what is it? The first order of business was to clear my head and stop drinking. I was about ready to go out on another maneuver that would last for three weeks at which time would be the right time to clear my thoughts and open my eyes to what may be out there wait- ing for me.

The field problem was long and hard but it did clear my mind and thoughts. I sat in my room reading a book when Tony walked in. He told me that his girlfriend had a friend that she would like me to meet. I really do not like blind dates but after a while, he talked me into it. It was going to be a lunch date within the next week. The more I thought about it the more intriguing the idea was.

· · · · · · ●●● ● ●●● · · · · · ·

Later that week, the duty roster was posted. My name appeared on it for staff duty. Staff duty was a twenty-four-hour watch of the Battalion checking barracks and security checks of the arms rooms. It was the day before my lunch date. I was not going to change the date for any reason. I would finish my tour of duty at 9:00 a.m. and the date was for 12:00. I knew that I was going to be tired but I would be able to sleep later. I have gone many hours without sleep thanks to the army.

The day arrived for my lunch date. I finished my staff duty and headed to my room to take a shower and change my clothes. I was very excited. I wanted to know how this was going to turn out. I left my room and headed out to the class six to pick up a nice bottle of wine.

I picked out a nice bottle of Chardonnay and headed for the front gate. I was supposed to meet Tony at his house that was just a half mile outside the gate. My date would show up a little bit later when her bus came in from Seoul. I arrived at Toni's house. He and his girlfriend Insue welcomed me warmly. I began to ask many questions about my date. I found out that, her name was Misun and that she was twenty-one years old. She worked down in Seoul as a secretary and that she would be here as soon as she could.

It was a two and a half hour buss ride. I was now thirty; I hope that she did not mind the age difference.

It was now 12:15, and we where starting to get worried. A few minutes later, there was a knock on the door. Tony went to answer the door. My heart started to pound and I started to feel very nervous for the first time in a very long time.

As the door opened, I look up to see a very attractive woman standing 5'7" tall wearing a long black dress. Her hair was very long and straight. She filled the room with a sweet scent of perfume that I have not ever encountered before. She was truly breath taking. I felt that I was staring at her for hours. She was beautiful. When her eyes meet mine for the first time, it seemed as if a flash of light passed right through me. I had never felt this before. I was com- pletely numb but I felt warm and comfortable. It was at this moment that I felt that this was why I was here. There was one question that I had to answer and that was how was I going to make her believe that my intensions where true.

Misun spoke very little English but that was okay because I could understand a lot of the Korean language but had trouble speaking it properly. We spent the after- noon talking and getting to know each other.

The day turned into night and we continued to talk. We sat next to each other the whole time and neither one of us feeling uncomfortable at any time. We all kind of missed lunch and mostly snacked, so we ordered dinner. We all sat around the table talking and eating. We drank the wine that I had brought with our dinner.

After dinner, we continued to talk. I was lost in time and space when my friend told me that it was now 1:00 a.m. I did not want this night to end. I was having such a great time but still there is a 2:00 a.m. curfew and I must get ready to head back to post. I wanted to say so much more but that would have to wait until next time.

I slowly got up from the floor and helped her up as well. She said that she would stay here and would later leave after she had some sleep. She wanted to walk me to the front gate but I told her that I would feel better if she would stay here. We agreed that she would walk to the end of the street. I said good-bye to Toni and Insue, I thanked them for a wonderful time.

Misun and I walked out the door, down the street; we had reached the end of the street and the ending of a beautiful day. She thanked me for coming to meet with her. I told her that it was my pleasure to be able to meet her and that I had an incredible day with her. I asked her if I could kiss her. She said yes. This was our first kiss not of passion but of respect for each other. It was not a long or deep kiss but a kiss that was brief as if requesting more.

After I kissed her, I said something that totally surprised her and I did not understand what I said until I was walk- ing through the gate. I told her that I could never like her. I know that left her with mixed feelings. I realized what I had said but I never finished the sentence. I meant to say that all I could do was love her. I felt so bad. I wanted to go back but it was too late and I hoped that I will be able to finish the sentence next time if there was going to be a next time.

I walked all the way back to my room calling myself an idiot. I could only pray that there will be a next time.

The next day, I could not stop thinking about her. I just had to see her again. I was going to Toni's house tonight and see if there was a way that we meet again. Work seemed to take far longer then days past. Not even the staff duty seemed as long. Finally, it was time to go clean up and head out to Toni's house.

I reached Toni's door and was meet by Insue who yelled at me for telling Misun that I could never like her. I now knew the impact that a messed up message sent. I felt like a complete fool. I told Insue that I never finished the sen- tence and that I did not realize this until it was too late. I wanted to tell her that I could only love her. If given the opportunity once again I will tell her myself if she will see me again. She smiled at me and said, so you want to see her again? I told her that I would like to see Misun as soon as possible because I cannot stop thinking about her.

Insue called Misun and told her that I wanted to see her again. Misun was shocked that I wanted to see her again. Misun asked her why I wanted to see again after I said what I did. She told Misun that he would have to explain it again; when you see him and that, he meant to say some- thing else. Misun said that she would not be able to get back there to see for another week. She was busy at work and could not get away. She told Misun that would be fine and she will see her than. They said something in Korean that I could not understand. They knew that I was listening in on the conversation but they knew that I was listening the whole time. With a laugh and closing good-byes, she hung up the phone.

After she hung up the phone, she explained everything to me and laughed at me because she knew I was listening the whole time. She told me that this is my last chance and I had better not mess it up this time. I nodded my head and thanked her for calling Misun for me.

I took her and Tony out to dinner that night. I was feeling much better now that I knew that she was going to come out and see me again. I will just have to be patient until then.

The next weekend, I went over to Toni's at a scheduled time that was set during the week. I knocked on the door and Misun answered it. I was at a loss for words. All I could manage at the time was a hello. I had not expected to see her when I arrived. I asked her later how she got there so soon she just smiled and said that she took the early bus.

We all talked for a while then I wanted to talk to Misun alone. Therefore, I asked her if she would like to go out for a walk. She said that she would love too. We walked all the way to second market where we enjoyed shopping and buying some food that we decided to cook together. At one point, I stopped her and told her what I really wanted to say that night and I felt bad on what I said. She smiled at me and said that she was very happy because she enjoyed being around me. She took my hand into hers and I turned her toward me and kissed her. This kiss was not like the first, this kiss it was just a little more deeper and enjoyable. We hugged each other and turned around holding hands to finish shopping.

Once back at Toni's house, I helped Misun cook dinner. Misun showed me what needed to be done. I do know my way around a kitchen but I never attempted to cook Korean food. This was to be a new first for me. I would say a first of many only if I do not open mouth and insert my foot again. The food was wonderful and was delightful to eat. After dinner was over, I helped her with the dishes. We went back out to the living room. Misun said that she had to be going soon. She had to work the next day and need to catch the bus back to Seoul. I felt crushed that she had to leave so soon. She was the one that decided to spend her off time with me.

It was now time for her to go; I was going to walk her to the bus station. We held hands and talked the whole way to the bus station. Her buss will soon be here and I did not want this moment to end. I stood there holding her until the bus arrived. As the bus pulled up, I looked down to her and kissed her just like in the market. I told her that I would miss her until I see her once again. She smiled and said that the days that we have been together were happi- est days she has had in a long time and she too would miss me until then. One quick kiss was all we could do before she boarded the bus. As she boarded the bus, I watched her move along the seats until she found one close to a win- dow as if to see me once more. I smiled and waved and she smiled and waved as the bus drove off.

I walked back to Toni's house and I felt like a high school boy in love for the very first time. I was walking among the clouds, feeling wonderful.

I stayed and talked with Tony and Insue for a while. He asked me when I was going to see Misun again. I forgot to ask her. I felt like such a fool again. He laughed at me and said that they will help me out again.

Misun and I went out on a few more dates. We enjoyed each other's company and loved shopping together. I told her that I had to leave for the field in the next few days and that I would be gone for about three weeks. She had understood the army life and said that she would be here when I came back. I smiled and promised that I would take her dancing when I returned. She said that we will go to a Korean club that she knows of and it will be fun. I smiled bent down to kiss her before she boarded the bus back to Seoul.

The whole three weeks I was in the field I could not get her off my mind. She filled every thought of every waking moment. Everyone asked me if I was feeling all right by other people. They told me that I was acting a little funny and smiled excessively. I could not tell them that I finally meet someone who fills my days, so I just kept smiling and said that I was fine.

I returned from the field and the first chance that I have to go down town, I would be on the first buss heading to main gate. I could not wait to talk to Misun.

To my surprise, she was already at Toni's house. My heart started to race. How could she know that I was going to be here today? I was not supposed to see her until tomorrow. I just thought I might be able to talk to her on the phone but this is even far better. Tony told me to say hello or something and stop staring into space.

Misun smiled. She said that she missed me and that she moved to TDC while I was in the field. I asked her why she had moved. I found out that this was a very stupid question to ask because Tony smacked in the back of my head and said that she moved her for you stupid. We all laughed and spent the rest of the night talking.

I walked Misun home. It was not far from Toni's house. She asked me if I wanted to come in. I was not sure if this was the right thing to do but I could not help myself. I went into her house. Her apartment was nice and only had a few things in it. I know she just moved in a few days ago because there were still some boxes were still in a corner not opened. Misun place was small but cozy. We sat on the floor and talked for a little while. I felt very comfortable sitting here with her. It was nice to be alone. We talked about our families and our past lives. It was very late by now and I really had to go. I did not want to leave. I did have a pass for the night but it was only just, in case she arrived late from Seoul. I got up and was getting ready to leave when she asked me if I wanted to stay. I so wanted to say okay but I knew that it was not right yet. I told her that I should go. She took a hold of my arm and said please. I could not say no now. I decided to stay.

We decided to celebrate so we went to a store and bought a bottle of Champagne. It was Korean made but it would be fine. Once back at her apartment, I opened the bottle of champagne. We drank a few glasses and Misun went into the kitchen and brought out some fruit to eat. We finished the bottle and some of the fruit. I reached over to her and kissed her. She gave herself to me that night. I would never forget it.

A few weeks later, she asked me to move in with her. She wanted to take care of me. I wanted to take care of her too. She still worked down in Seoul and was often very tired when she came home, I asked her to quite her job and that I would take care of her. She was very happy. I moved in a few days later. I still had to keep a room on post but I was able to go home to Misun almost every night.

I came home from work on night to find that Mrs. Lee was there. I was nervous. I said hello in Korean and bowed to her just as their customs. Mrs. Lee just smiled and took my hand. She led me into the apartment. We all sat down at the small table. Mrs. Lee got up from the table and went into the kitchen. She brought out a lot of food. It smelled so good. We all ate and drank some beer together. I really enjoyed her mothers company. We talked about Misun and me going down to meet her father next week. I was sure that it would be fine and that I would take a pass to go. Mrs. Lee had to go. She did not want to miss the train. We all got up and went to the train station. I said good-bye and she got on the train.

On the way home, Misun told me that I needed to learn some Korean customs if I were to meet with her father. She told me that he was very traditional. I told her that I would be happy to learn them.

Misun taught me many of the customs. I told Misun that I was not going to speak to her father as to make a wrong impression. My Korean was not that good. If I said something wrong, I know that it would leave a bad impression. I asked Misun to translate for me. Misun told me that I would be the first American that her family ever met. I knew from this day forward I was under a lot of pressure.

The day had arrived; Misun and I boarded a train head- ing to see her family. It was a two-hour train ride and a fifteen-minute taxicab ride. I was very nervous. I was not able to eat all day, I was that nervous. We got out of the taxi and walked up to the house. It was on the second floor.

I took a deep breath and prayed that I did not mess this up. We knocked on the door and Mrs. Lee answered it. She greeted me and pulled me into the house. I first meet Mrs. Yi. She was a very nice older woman and very nice to me. She was Misuns Grandmother. She took me into a room and I sat there. Misun had to explain, it was custom that the quest would stay in a room and wait to be greeted by everyone. I was not to leave and family members would come into the room to greet me. I would have to bow to all of them except for the children. She had to help her mother in the kitchen and she would check up on me from time to time. I did not know that I would meet her entire family. I only thought that I would meet her father, brothers and mother. I had no idea. This was overwhelming but I had to do this for Misun.

I spent the next six hours greeting all of the relatives that came over. I left once to go to the restroom. I really enjoyed Mrs. Yi. She was very cool. She always came into see me and asked me if I needed anything. She knew that my Korean was not very good, but that did not matter to her. She told me not to bow to her every time she entered the room. It was not necessary for her. She was the eldest of the family and always had the last word. No one disre- spected her no matter what. I learned this through Misun. It was now dinnertime. Misun brought me out of the room and sat down at the table. It was a large table and it was full of food. The food smelled so good and looked delightful. I was ready to eat. They placed a spoon next to my bowl of rice. I do not think that they knew that I could use chopsticks very well. It was custom for me to pour the drinks. I had to wait to drink any alcohol until someone older than I offered it to me. Mrs. Yi was the one who offered me a drink. I accepted the drink. The food was very delicious. I wanted to eat more but I did not want Misun family to think that I was a pig or something else.

After dinner, all of the family except for Mrs. Lee and father left. We all sat on the couch and talked. Misun translated for me. The hard part was over now. I could be normal without having to worry about formalities. We all were just normal people. I still wanted to have Misun translate for me.

We talked about my intensions toward their daughter. I said that I loved her very much and would do anything to keep her safe and happy. I told them that my intensions were to marry Misun. I asked Mr. Lee for Misuns hand in marriage. He looked at me and asked me a question. He said a man and women have two levels in a relationship if we rate them on a scale from one to ten, the man is a seven and the women are a three. How would you rate yourself and my daughter? I said that in a relationship between a man and a woman should be equal to each other. We would share in our ideas and affairs. We would need to be equal because no one person could dominate the other and both are happy. It would still be my responsibility to support her and our children. The women would need to grow and would need to be independent to make choices for her. My father helped me understand this when I was growing up. I hold many of his values in life to this day. I offset this equal balance in a relationship by placing her needs and the needs off the children first. Once their needs are satisfied then I would be able to take care of mine.

Mrs. Lee was so happy to hear this she said something to her husband and he just smiled. Mr. Lee got up from the couch and went over to a wall where he had many bottles of *soju*. Each bottle had different things in them. Some had different kinds of ginseng and others had different types of fruit. He took a bottle from off the shelf and brought it over to the table. While he was pouring two drinks, He explained that he made each one. It was very rare that he would open a bottle for anyone. This occasion required a special bottle. Misun could not drink in front of her par- ents. This was their custom.

I drank with Mr. Lee most of the night. We talked and laughed together. At one point, I forgot to have Misun translate for me. It was the soju talking. Mr. Lee looked at me and laughed. He said that I spoke Korean like a child just learning to speak. I apologized for my Korean and asked for his forgiveness. He said that there was no need to apologize. Everything was fine. The rest of the night, Mr. Lee brought many different bottles from off the shelves. I think that he wanted to try them all in one night. I was feeling drunk by now and I know he was feeling it too. I could not stop; I did not want to insult him.

It was early morning now; it was time for Misun and me to go home. Mrs. Lee knew that we had to get back home. She told her husband that we had to go now. I was glad she intervened. We got up from the couch and walked toward the door. I was sure that I was going to make it home with Misuns help. It would be a long taxi ride home. The trains did not travel this time in the morning. We all walked out to the street, Misun and I proceeded to get into the taxi when her father handed Misun some money. I was going to object but Misun told me not to say or do anything. I thanked them for a wonderful day and told them that they needed to come to our place for dinner.

We drove off and talked about our day with her family. I guess that I made a good impression with her family except her eldest uncle. He did not like the idea of mixing cultures. Mrs. Yi intervened and told him to stay out of it. She told Misun's uncle that I was a good man and she had no problem with it. I also found out that if I were to marry Misun, I would be the eldest son and Mrs. Lee would have the responsibility of ensuring that Misun was taking care of me. This was her role and their custom. If Misun did not take care of me and if the mother let this happen, the rest of the family would look down upon her and her husband. I was shocked to hear this.

It took two and a half hours to get home. Misun and I were very tired. She paid the taxicab driver, and we got into our apartment and went to sleep.

· · · · · · · · · ● ● · · · · · · · · · ·

Two weeks later, Misun and I arranged for her immedi- ate family to come over for dinner. I would not be able to afford for all of her relations to come. Therefore, the only guests who were coming were her mother, father, brothers, and their wives. I wanted to make an American dish for them, so I decided to make my famous spaghetti. I knew that this was the right choice for dinner. Misun helped me out in the kitchen while I cooked. While we prepared din- ner, she told me of one of their customs: A Korean man never stepped foot in the kitchen. It was the wife's place, not the husband's. I told her that I would have to explain it to them when they arrived.

They all arrived at our house and went inside. They saw that I was in the kitchen. Misun's father asked her what I was doing there. She explained to him that I wanted to make dinner for all of us, that it was my custom to share in the responsibilities in the house. He accepted her answer, even if he clearly did not like it.

It was dinnertime. I brought out the spaghetti sauce, and Misun brought out the noodles and garlic bread. We used chopsticks instead of forks (but I had forks just in case).

They all had a strange look on their faces. I guess they did not know what to think of this meal. Misun showed them what they needed to do. Mr. Lee went first. He took a bite and instantly had this look of surprise. Then he shook his head and told the rest of the family that it was very good. We all sat at the table and ate dinner. I brought out a bottle of Chivas Regal whiskey. I thought that Mr. Lee would like it. I opened the bottle and poured him a drink. He liked the taste but said that compared to soju, it was not very strong. I told him that all American alcohol were of the same strength. He offered his glass to me and poured me a glass.

Everyone loved dinner. It was the first time that they ate anything that was not Korean. They could not stay very long because of work the next day. All the men talked while the women went into the kitchen and cleaned up. I knew I could not help. The women came out into the living room with a plate of fruit and placed it on the table. We all talked and ate some of it.

Misun got up from the table and walked into the kitchen. This was my chance to talk to her. I followed her into the kitchen, walked up to her, and kissed her. She said that she did not want her family to see us kissing. I understood and reached into my pocket. I pulled out a small box, opened it, and asked her to marry me. She was obviously shocked but said yes. Then I placed the ring on her finger. (Her father had given me permission when we went to her house.) She gave me a quick kiss and, out of excitement, asked her mother to come into the kitchen.

Mrs. Lee walked into the kitchen, and Misun showed her the ring. Mrs. Lee hugged me and took Misun into the living room to show everyone. I walked out into the living room and found that everyone was standing up. Mr. Lee walked over to me and shook my hand. His sons followed suit. The women were very happy for Misun and pulled her in for a hug. It was a very special day. Mr. Lee wanted to celebrate, so he decided that we were all to go out to a Korean club.

We all got into three taxis and headed to one of the Korean clubs close by. It was a very expensive club and only allowed entrance to Koreans. Mr. Lee talked to the manager, and I think that he gave him some money to let me in the club. We all sat at a large table, and Mr. Lee ordered some drinks and a large fruit plate. For the next few hours, we all danced and celebrated our engagement. Mr. Lee spent a lot of money that night.

It was getting late and the men had to go to work the next morning. It was time to go. We all walked out of the club and got into taxis. Misun and I were going home and the other went to their homes. We all said our good-byes and went home.

Misun and I went to visit her parents a few times. I spent most of my time in the field. We started to work on our marriage paperwork. We had no idea what it was going to take. We found out that it was going to cost a lot of money. There was going to be many officials from the American government as well as the Korean government to approve our paperwork. I went to work on the paperwork for the American side while Misun went to work on the Korean side. It took months for the paperwork to go through. We needed to go to the American embassy to have the final paperwork signed. We could not miss that day other wise we would have to wait even longer to reschedule it.

Our scheduled day was during my three-month tour for our unit to guard the DMZ. I talked with my commander and he allowed me a two-day pass to go to Seoul.

I signed out on pass and got on a bus to head for home. I met Misun at the bus station and we went home. I had been up on the DMZ for a month now and could have any visitors. I was glad to be home. Misun cooked me something to eat and we went to bed.

We woke up early the next morning to get ready to travel to Seoul. Misun explained what we needed to do. There were a few places that we had to go before we had to go to the US Embassy. It was a long train and taxicab ride.

We spent half the day going to the other places and now it was time to go to the US Embassy. It was now lunchtime so we decided to get something to eat. We ate a little shop that was just outside the US Embassy.

After lunch, we walked into the US Embassy with all of our paperwork signed. We dropped off our paperwork at a window and took a seat. Misun and I sat there for about three hours. Finally, a woman at the window called our names. Misun and I walked over to the window. The women looked over our paperwork and pulled out a stamp. She stamped our paperwork and congratulated us. We were now married in the eyes of both governments.

We were very happy walking out of the Embassy. Mrs. Lee was waiting for us out side the large gates. We all took a taxi to the train station and boarded a train heading for Mrs. Lees house.

When we arrived at her house, Mr. Lee and brother were there. We all sat down at the table and had some- thing to eat. I told my now father-in-law that I could not drink any alcohol because I had to go back to the DMZ later that night. He understood and said that there will be another time.

It only seemed a few minutes had passed before I had to leave. I so wish that I had more time. I was lucky I was able to have as much time as I did. We all said our good-byes, Misun, and I headed for train station. We stopped at TDC where we lived and walked over to the buss station. I kissed

my new bride good-bye and boarded a bus to the DMZ…
Memories, I have so many and so little time to remem- ber
them all. I smiled to my self then the nurse walked into
the room with my breakfast. She left reminding me to eat
everything today. I said thank you and that I would try as
she walked out the door.

I ate very little and decided to sleep some more. I was
growing very weary and tired. I know that I will have visitors later and I would need to conserve my strength for
them. I laid my head back on my pillow and soon fell asleep.

5

I departed my plane, picked up my bag, and headed for the rental cars counter. I forgot to make a reservation for a car, but I figured that I would be able to rent a car here in Fayetteville. I walked up to the counter and asked the woman at the counter if there were cars for rent. She said that she had a Mustang and a Focus; that was all. I began to laugh. The mention of a Mustang brought back a funny memory that I had.

Bryan told me once when we were out looking for a car for me that I would look better driving a red Mustang convertible than a red Camry. I, of course, chose the Camry. I looked at the woman at the counter, still smiling, and chose the Mustang. I handed her my credit card and signed the paperwork. She gave me back my card and the keys to the rental Mustang.

I walked out of the airport and over to where the cars were parked. There was a big van in front of my rental. I walked around the van and noticed that the Mustang was red, and it was a convertible. I thought that this had become too uncanny just to be mere coincidence. I opened the door and got in the car. The first thing that I did was put the top down. I only did this once before while driving my friend's car. It was nice driving with the wind in my face.

I needed to find a motel and check into a room. I have not been in Fayetteville for some time, but I remembered that the best place to find a motel was around the mall. While driving toward the mall, I noticed a small bookstore. I pulled into the parking lot and parked the car. Then I proceeded to enter the store.

I walked to the counter and asked the man at the counter if he had a copy of *The Necklace* by Bryan McIntire. He said that he had only a hardback copy left. I told him that, that would be fine. I purchased the book and went back to the car. I left the parking lot and headed for the mall. I noticed that Fayetteville had changed since I was here last. There were many more restaurants and stores. There were also condominiums everywhere.

I saw the Holiday Inn and decided to find a room there. I pulled into the parking lot and parked the car. I walked into the hotel and over to the front counter. I asked the woman if there was a room to rent. She asked me for how many nights would I be staying. I told her that I would be staying for three days. I asked her if they still had the bar downstairs. She told me that it was now a nightclub and it opens at 7:00 p.m. I thanked her.

I remembered that Bryan used to bring me here once in a while, and every time, we danced and had a few drinks. We had a good time.

The woman at the counter asked me, "How would you be paying? Cash or charge?"

I told her, "Charge."

I took out my wallet from my purse and handed her my card along with my driver's license. She handed me my card and the key card for my room. She told me where to find my room and where to park my car. (My room number was 124.) I then thanked her and headed for the car.

I got into the car and drove around the building toward my room. I parked my car and put the top back up. I got my suitcase from the trunk and headed to my room. I opened the door and walked into the room. It was a nice room and looked quite comfortable. There was a cable TV with several channels, a small stereo, a table with two chairs, and a queen-size bed. In the back of the room was a closet, and next to it was a small counter with a small coffeepot on it. I knew that would come in handy later. At the end of the counter was the bathroom. This was going to be my first stop. I needed to take a shower.

I would not be able to see Bryan until later because I knew that his family would be there, and I did not want to get into any confrontation with anyone. After I left, his family did not like me. His mother hated me for what I did to him. I do understand their feelings decided to stay away.

His oldest sister lived in Texas while the rest of his family lived in California. I knew that his oldest sister was prob- ably staying at his house and taking care of the kids. He once told me that if anything were to happen to him, she was the one who'll watch over them, and I agreed.

As for his mom and dad, I think that they would stay at his house as well. Even though his sister and mother did not agree on things, I hope that they would have peace for now. The rest of the family were going to be at a hotel close by. *I hope that they are not at* this *hotel. I do not want to run into any of them right now.* I looked over to the clock on the table and noticed that it was already 4:30 p.m. It was time to clean up and call Insuk to let her know that I made it okay and that I would go down to the hospital later after his family left. I really wanted to see him, but I was going to have to wait.

I called Insuk and told her that everything was okay and that I needed the name of the hospital where Bryan was staying. She said that he was at Cape Fear in room 508. I told her that I was going to take a shower and get some- thing to eat before I headed off to the hospital. She told me that she hoped that everything was all right and that she hoped that she would get the chance to see me before she left. Insuk lived in Charlotte, which was about three hours away. I told her that I hoped to see her too and then said good-bye. I put the phone down, opened my suitcase, and hung my clothes in the closet. It was now time for a shower.

After I took a shower, I remembered that I had bought Bryan's book. I decided to read some of its pages. I heard that his book was very good and that it had been a best seller for a few months. I could never read it back then because Bryan had told me that it contained a lot of our history together and that it would bring back too many memories. However, I did not have a choice now but to read it.

I went out to the car and got the book from the passenger's seat. I went back into the room, lay on the bed, and started reading the book. As I read the book, it was like reading my past life with Bryan. It was well written and very true. It brought back so many memories, and it made me begin to cry. I felt his pain and his sadness. I put the book down and cried 'til I fell asleep.

I was dreaming of the day I said good-bye, when I drove off with Miyon.

Miyon and I were heading for Virginia for a business proposal with one of her friends. It was late in the afternoon when we got to her friend's house. I was still thinking of Rachel and Junior, Bryan and Kevin. I was a little confused. *Maybe the time here will help me sort this entire problem.*

We all ate and talked over this deal. It sounded too good to be true and seemed to be a catch, but they did not say what it was. Tomorrow we were all going to go over the numbers and decide what to do.

I bought a pay-as-you-go phone when we left Bryan's house so I could call the kids when I wanted. I called them,

let them know I was okay, and told them that I loved them. I asked them where was Bryan they told me that he was in the shower and getting ready for bed. They told me that they had to go to bed soon because they had to go to school tomorrow.

I look at the clock. It was 9:30 p.m. I talked to Rachel and told her to give my phone number to Bryan. She told that she would. She asked me if I wanted dad to call her when he got out of the shower. I told her that was not necessary and that I would call him later. I told her I loved her and that I would talk to her later. I ended the call and decided to call Kevin.

I have not talked to Kevin in over a week. I knew he was out on a mission but I did not know how long he was going to be gone or where he went. I dialed his number and to my surprise, he answered. We talked over and hour. We laughed and said some silly things.

He asked me how my visit with kids went and I told him that everything was great and that the kids are so grown up. I proceeded to tell him what we did and where we went but he said that he was tired and had to get a few things done. I really did not want him to cut me off like that but I think that he was a little jealous of the kids. He told me that he loved me and that he hoped to see me soon.

He also said that he had some news for me but that it was not the time. I told him that I loved him too and that I would call tomorrow if that were okay. He said that would be fine. I ended that call and just sat there in the chair star-ing out the window. I knew that I had to make up my mind soon on what I was going to do. I could never tell Bryan about Kevin, nor could I ever tell Kevin that I slept with my ex-husband either. I had a big problem.

The next day, I found out that the proposition was not what we where looking for. It was going to a restaurant business. Miyon friends where going to invest most of the money but we had to come up with the rest. We did not have the money to invest in this deal. We talked some more they where going to open a restaurant no matter what. They told us that we could work there once it opened if we wanted. It was not really what Miyon and I wanted. We decided to stay one more night and then we would figure out what to do next.

That night I talked with Miyon and told her that we should try to find something in North Carolina so we could be closer to our children. She agreed and we would head for North Carolina in the morning. Miyon asked if I knew of anyone that we could stay with for a few days because a hotel was very expensive. I told her that I would call Bryan and ask if it was okay for us to stay there. I knew Bryan would say yes. I really did not want to impose on him with my friend but I still would ask.

I called Bryan and asked him if Miyon and I could stay at his house for a little while and that, we where going to find work and be closer to our kids. Bryan was very happy and told us that there was no problem with it. He would fix up Junior's room for Miyon and place Junior in with Rachel. He then asked when we would be coming. I asked him if tomorrow was okay. He told me that would be great. I got of the phone with Bryan and told Miyon the news. She was happy and asked me what I was going to do about Kevin. I looked at her and said that I was not sure.

I decided to call Kevin. I spoke with him and found out what his news was. He had papers reassigning him to Ft. Lewis Washington. I was there once with Bryan. I asked him when he has to leave. He told that it was going to be a few weeks before that would take place and that he had to attend a school at Ft. Bragg, North Carolina, first. I told him that I would be going back to North Carolina in the morning and was going to find some work. I also told him that I would be staying with a friend. He said that this might work out great. He asked me what I wanted to do with my things in Korea. I did not have very many things and so I asked him if there was any way that he could bring them to North Carolina and that I would call my friend in Korea and she would take the furniture. He said that would be fine. He said that he loved me and could not wait to see me. I told him that I loved him too. We said our good byes and I ended the call. Miyon was in the room at this time. She asked me what I was going to do. I told her I did not know. We will have to see when I get to North Carolina.

The next morning we left for North Carolina. It was not a very long drive and I drove the whole way. Miyon was getting a little carsick and so we had to make a few stops on the way. I called Bryan to see if he was at home. He was at home and told me that He had to go back to work very soon. He asked me how far away I was from his house. I told him that I would be another twenty minutes before I get there. Bryan said that he would have to leave and that he would leave the key in the mailbox before he left. He told me that Miyon's room was ready and there was plenty of food and things in the kitchen. He said that the kids where very happy that I was going to stay with them for a while and that they would be getting home around 3:00

p.m. He said that he would not be home until 5:30 p.m. I am to make myself at home. Bryan said that he had to go because he had to finish getting ready for work. He told me that he would see me later today and told me that it was nice that I decide to come home for a while and that he loved me. I told him it was nice of him to let Miyon to stay and that I love him too. He said good-bye and hung up the phone. I ended the call and Miyon just looked at me and told me that I was playing with fire. I told her I knew what I was doing and that I was going to fix everything.

Miyon and I stayed at Bryans for about a week when Miyon told me that she had to leave. She was very upset with me and wanted to go home. The night before we had an argument about how I was playing with Bryan and Kevin, I was sleeping with Bryan, calling Kevin every night when Bryan was asleep, and telling him that I loved him too. Bryan setup an internet email account for me and showed me how to use it. He gave me free access to the computer and when he was at work, I would email Kevin.

I was working a t a restaurant down the street and Miyon wanted to go back home to Colorado. She found out that her ex-husband was getting married in a few months. She was not happy. She said that she was leaving tomorrow morning and that she would call me when she made it home. Bryan was in the other room sitting on the couch with the kids watching TV. Miyon and I came out of Junior's room and we told them that Miyon was going back home to Colorado. She was leaving in the morning. Bryan asked was there was anything that he could do. She smiled and told him that he had already done more then he should have and thanked him for letting her stay.

Miyon left the next morning. I felt very sad for her and really did not want her to leave. She was still mad at me for playing this game and wanted no part of it. She reminded me that Bryan was a very good man and that I had a second chance to make it right. Miyon did not have a second chance her time had already passed. She hugged me before she left and told me to do the right thing.

A week had passed and everything was going fine until one day Bryan came home early. I was reading an email from Kevin when he drove up in the driveway. I panicked and hit different key to shut down the computer. I do not no what I did but the computer just locked up. Rachel looked at me and told me that daddy was not going to be very happy. I told Rachel to go into the living room and watch TV. Bryan just walked through the front door as I got up from the computer, I could do nothing. I met him at the entrance to his room. He said hello and kissed me. I told him that I was sorry I did something to his computer because it is not working anymore. He said that he would look at it. I told him that I was sorry. He told me not to worry he would be able to fix it. He went into the room, sat down on the computer, and started to work on it.

It took about twenty minutes for him to fix the computer and he got up and said that it was fine now. He was holding a piece of paper in his hand. I asked him what it was. He just said that it was a jammed paper in the printer. I was very worried about what I just did. It was getting out of hand now. I still did not know what to do. Kevin was coming to

North Carolina in a few weeks for school and he wanted to take me with him to Ft. Lewis, Washington. I was not sure what to do.

For the next few days, I played it very cool. I did not email Kevin; I just called him late at night. Bryan has been working very late and he helped me to get a car. He did not have to do this but he wanted to. One night Bryan came over to talk with me. He had just put the kids to bed. We where sitting down on the couch. He had a piece of paper in his hand. I had no Idea what it was. I found out soon enough. He handed me the paper and explained how he received it. It was a copy of Kevin's email to me. The very one that I was reading the day he came home early. He also told me that he email Kevin and asked him what he wanted to do. Kevin and Bryan both agreed that it was my choice. Bryan was a little upset with me because of all of this. He told me that he would have helped me even if he had known about Kevin. He said that I would have to give him an answer by tomorrow. He told me that I could have the bed and that he was going to sleep on the couch. I told him that I was sorry about all of this and I should have said something a long time ago. He looked at me walked outside.

I knew that I just crushed him once again. I was playing a deadly game, now I was caught. Miyon told me this was going to happen and I thought that I had it under control. I called Kevin and talked with him. He was a little mad at me and wanted to know if I had decided what I was going to do. I told him that I decided to go with him to Washington. I would find a place here, move out, and wait for him. He asked if I talked with Bryan yet. I told him not yet.

Bryan walked back into the house after a thirty-minute walk. I told him of my decision and asked him if he was going to be okay. Bryan said that they would be fine but I was going to be the one to tell the kids. I agreed to tell them. The next morning was a beautiful Saturday morning. I woke up to the smell of coffee, eggs, bacon and toast. I got up from the bed and went into the living room. Bryan was cooking breakfast while the kids where watching morning cartoons. Bryan handed me a cup of coffee and told me that breakfast will be done in a few minutes.

We all sat at the table and ate breakfast. Bryan finished his breakfast first, picked up his plate, and went into the kitchen. I was almost done eating and the kids where finished. They got up from the table, went into the kitchen,

and handed Bryan their dishes. Bryan took their dishes and they ran off into the living room to watch TV. I finished my breakfast, walked over to the kitchen, and gave Bryan my dishes. I asked him if I could help him. He told me that he is almost finished and that he had it covered. I then noticed he was no longer wearing his wedding ring. I wanted to ask him why but I knew why and did not want to push it any farther. I went into the living room and sat next to the kids.

I decided that this would be the best time to tell them. I told the kids that I was moving out and that they could come over to visit me whenever they wanted. They where hurt and asked why I had to move out. I told them that Bryan and I had a little problem and it was best that I move out. Bryan walked into the living room at this time. The kids noticed he was standing there and begged him to let mommy stay here. He told the kids that there was no choice in this matter. Bryan was taking all of the pres- sure off me and placing it on himself. The kids where very upset and hugged me crying saying please do not leave us mommy. I was tearing me apart. Bryan was the one who spoke first. Bryan told the kids to give their mom a kiss and to go to there rooms and get dressed. We are going to help your mom look for a nice place to live. They tried to make a fuss but Bryan stopped it before it started. In a firm tone of voice he said, "Now, go!" The kids did not question his words they went to their rooms.

We all went looking for an apartment and found one that was not to far from the house. It was half way between Ft. Bragg and Bryan's house. It would take about ten to fifteen minutes from Bryan's house depending on traffic. Bryan helped with getting the electricity and water turned on. I would be able to move in on Monday morning. Bryan told me that I could have a pick of the furniture in the house but his bed was not an option. I knew that he was not going to give up his bed for anything. I picked out a few things and told Bryan what I needed and he would help me move.

Monday was a training holiday for Bryan. He decided that the kids would stay home and help with the moving. He had to go into work for PT and the nine o'clock for- mation, but he would return home after that. Bryan came home at around ten and was ready to help me move in. We loaded up the truck and my car then headed for the apart- ment. We moved everything into the apartment and Bryan added a few things to the list of items that I wanted. We placed everything where I wanted them and Bryan setup a TV with a VCR for the kids. He told me that I could have them and I would need them for when the kids came over, there where also some tapes for the kids and some mov- ies for me to watch. After we set up the apartment, Bryan asked me if I wanted to watch the kids for a little while so they would get used to the apartment. I told him that I would love to do that and that I would bring them home before I had to go to work. I told Bryan that I needed to go get some groceries for the kids and myself but he told me to look and see what I needed first. I thought that I needed everything. I did not notice that Bryan also brought in some groceries from his house and placed them where they needed to go. I went into the kitchen and noticed them. I thanked him for everything. He told the kids that he had to go home and that I would take them home before I went to work. They hugged Bryan and gave him a kiss. Bryan came over to me, took my hand, and told me that he would see me later. I wanted to kiss him to thank him for everything but I know that he was hurting and this was for the best.

I spent the day with the kids and it was time for me to take them home now, they where ready to go home and I needed to go to work.

I dropped of the kids at Bryans and he told me to stop by the house when I got off work. He had something that he wanted to give me. I told him I would come over after work.

After work, I went over to Bryan's house. I walked over to the door and rang the doorbell. I never had to do this before but it seemed to be the right thing to do. I felt a little awkward. Bryan opened the door and told me that I could have just walked in. He was expecting me and we did not need to go through the formalities. I walked in the house and noticed that the kids were already asleep. Bryan was in the living room drinking a beer and watching the TV. He asked me to sit down.

We talked for a while and I found out that he had to leave the army. He loved the army but he had a temporary job and was trying to make this temporary job a permanent one. He could not do his old job because he was a single parent and it required a lot of field time. He never told me this until now. This was going on for the last four weeks. He told me that the Army denied his request and that he had to return to his old job. He told me that he was given a choice his career or his kids. He told me that he did not even hesitate and told them he was going home to raise his kids and that the paperwork he needed will be in on Monday. He told me that it would take them a few weeks to process the paperwork and he would soon be out of the Army. Bryan had been in the Army for fifteen years and I know that he would have wanted to stay in and retire at twenty years but the army forced his hand and the only choice he could for his kids. When he told me all of this, I felt so sorry for him. I turned his life upside down.

Bryan did something that I would have never expected of him. He reached under the pillow that was on the couch, pulled out a small box, and handed it to me. He told me that this was for me and he would explain it once I opened it. I took the box. It was rectangular with black velvet on the outside. I was a jewelry box. I told him that I could not accept it. He told me that I had too. He had it made just for me. I was very shocked by what he just said. I opened the box and to my surprise was a beautiful necklace inside. There was a gold band for the medallion with a crystal piece placed in the center. In the center of that was a beau- tiful red ruby. There were two chains holding the medal- lion one was a box design and the other was of serpentine design. The chains ended in a lobster claw clasp. This neck- lace was beautiful. I have never seen one like this before. Bryan began to explain. He said that the medallion was his wedding band and he had a crystal placed in the center, He bought a bloodred Burmese ruby and had it placed in the center.

The jeweler had a hard time with it but I had a drawing of what I wanted and he said he would make it. He then told me that there was a lot of meaning behind this necklace and he would explain it as well. He began: the gold band represents our bond we shared, the crystal represents the purity of that bond, the ruby represents the love that we shared, the two necklaces represent different meanings first; the box chain represents the life that we shared and the serpentine chain represents the life that we have still yet to share. I did not understand it but Bryan loved symbol- ism in things he believed in. This necklace was amazing. I tried to give it back to him once again. I did not deserve this from anyone. Bryan said that when ever I felt sad or frightened just by wearing this necklace would bring me peace. He would not take it back for any reason and told me that it was just me and no one else. I reached over and kissed him.

Bryan never bought jewelry for me for many years. I had a bad habit of losing it. He bought me some very nice pieces but I just lost them. I remember when I lost my wedding band along with my engagement ring. Bryan knew that I lost them but would not confront me with it. I ended up telling him. He was a little mad when we went out and bought me a simple wedding band. I even lost that one a month later. He told me that he would never buy another piece of jewelry ever again until now.

He took the necklace and told me to turn around. I did as he requested. He put my hair to one side and placed the necklace around my neck. When the necklace touched my neck, it felt warm and soothing. I turned around and he told me it was perfect. I told him that I had to go look in the mirror. I went into the bathroom and looked into the mirror. The necklace looked as if had a glow to it but I never thought nothing of it. It looked more beautiful when I was wearing it. I went back to the living room, hugged, and kissed him once again. I told him that he never should have done this. He told me that he had to and it was the only way. I asked him what he meant by that. He just told me to never mind and that he was just being foolish.

We drank a beer or two together and it was time for me to go home. This was very strange when I think about it. This used to be my home and now I can never call it that ever again. Bryan walked me to the car and said goodnight. He did not walk into the house until I drove out of site.

For the next two weeks, I went to visit the kids and Bryan. I always wore the necklace. I had many people inquire about it and I told them the story except for its meaning. I knew that Bryan meant that for me only. They all loved it. I was very proud of it. Bryan was having a time with his paperwork. The army tried to have him reconsider his release but he told them that he had no other choice. They told him that someone could raise them when he was on deployments. He just told them that he would never let that happen because he was their father and he was com- mitted to raising them not anyone else. He finally got it all sorted out and was finally going to get his orders to out- processing the army.

I talked with Kevin every night and he told me that he would be in Fayetteville by weeks end. He was looking forward to seeing me and being with me once again. I was looking forward to seeing him once again as well. I asked him how long he had to go to school. He told me that it was on eight weeks long and we would have to leave for Ft. Lewis a day or so afterward. I told him that would be fine and that he could stay here at the apartment while he was going to school. He said that would be perfect.

The next day, I went over to Bryan's house and told him that Kevin would be here by weeks end. He was not thrilled about it but he knew he was coming. He asked me for one request and that it was that the kids could only visit with me when he was not around. He did not want the kids to get confused about Kevin. I did understand his meaning. The last month has been hard on the kids to have their mother show back up, then move out again, and if I brought Kevin into the picture it would surly confuse them. I agreed to the request.

Kevin showed up at weeks end as he said he would. I picked him up at the airport and took him home with me.

He said that he was going to rent a car so he could travel back and forth to Ft. Bragg. We had many things to catch up on. We were at home one evening and he asked me about the necklace. I told him that the kids had picked it out for me. He said that he had never seen a necklace like that before and it looked expensive. I told him that the kids wanted to get it for me and that Bryan said it was okay. We were sitting on the couch watching TV at the time. He moved closer to me and placed his hand on the necklace. He looked at it more closely. He said that it was unique and it was not a cheap piece of jewelry. He said that he did not like it because it was too simple for his taste. This was the first time that he rejected to something that I was wearing but he would never ask me to take it off unless we were in bed.

I did not get to see the kids as often as I wanted too. I told Kevin abut the request that Bryan asked me about the kids seeing him with me. He told me that was for the best and that Bryan was probably right.

Time seemed to slip by because it was already time for Kevin and me to go to Ft. Lewis. I had never told the kids about me leaving. I did not even tell them I was getting married again to another man. I just kept putting it off and now it is too late. I told Kevin that I was going over to Bryan's house to tell the kids good-bye. He told me that we were to leave in the morning. I told him that I would not be long. I gathered up all of the kid's toys and tapes and put them into boxes. I had a few other things for them that I found when we were packing that I wanted them to have. I packed them in the car and headed for Bryan's house.

I drove up into the driveway and parked the car. I got out of the car and stood there staring at the house. I knew that I would never see it again. I walked up to the door and the kids were already coming out. They ran over to me and hugged me. I bent down and kissed both of them. To my surprise, they asked if it was time for me to leave again. By now, Bryan was standing there. I asked them what you mean. They told me that Bryan told them that I had to move far away so she could make lots of money to buy presents for them and that she would call them and write to them. They started to feel bad by the sound of me leav- ing again. Bryan told them first and softened the blow. I told them that what their dad said was true and that I had to go. I told them to be good and to take care of Bryan for me. We began to cry together. I hugged them and kissed them. I had something's in my car that belonged to them and asked them if they could help me carry them into the house. We all went over to the car and took the boxes out. There where a few gifts that I had bought for the kids and they were excited to open them. I thanked Bryan for telling the kids for me and that I had completely forgot all about it. He said it was no problem.

I had only a few more minutes to spare with the kids. I was lost in thought because I did not know if I was going to be able to see them again. I did not know what to expect on this new adventure or new life. I became frightened. I think Bryan knew something because he walked over to me and put his arms around me and said that it will be okay. If I ever needed help, I knew his phone number to call day or night. I hugged him and thanked him once again. I walked over to the kids and told them it was time for me to go now. They hugged and kissed me and told me that they loved me. I told both of them that I loved them and will miss them and to be good for Bryan. I stood up, walked over to the car, and got in. I did not want to fall apart. Bryan closed the car and told me to take care. I could not say anything I just waved my hand and drove off…

I woke up in the hotel room feeling very sad and a little confused. The only dreams that I have had were of my memories with Bryan. I moved the book from off my chest and turned over to look at the clock on the table. I read 8:15 p.m. It was getting late, and I had to get up and go to the hospital. I got up, went over to the counter, and made a cup of coffee. It was instant of course but it will have to do for now. I was a little hungry but that would have to wait until later. I took out my toothbrush from my suitcase, brushed my teeth, and washed my face. I put on some make up but not a lot. I did not want to look like I just woke up. I got dressed and drank my cup of coffee. I was soon out the door and headed for the hospital.

6

Bryan was deep in thought when he felt a familiar presence in the room. He turned his head over and looked toward the door. There she stood as beautiful as the first day they met it was Misun. Bryan was speechless. She was the first one to break the silence. As she walked over to him, she tried to smile trying to hide her tears.

"I am sorry that I didn't walk in earlier but your family was here and I did not want to get in the way. I know how your family feels about me, so I stayed in the shadows until they left. Rachel and Junior are sure getting big. I want to see them but I must attend to your needs first," she said.

"You are just as beautiful as the day we meet. So what brings you to North Carolina?" Bryan asked.

Misun smiled because Bryan had a way with words, she replied, "I had heard that you where sick and that I need to be here."

Bryan thanked her for coming all this way to see him and that he was very happy to see her again. He noticed that she was wearing the necklace that he had made for her two years ago. It seemed to be glowing. He asked her about it and she said that it was the reason why she was here. She said the necklace told her not in word but with a sense or feeling that there was something wrong and I needed to come.

She began to tell him of her events over the last few hours. When she told him about the flashes and images that she had received, he was shocked. He could not believe this but he let her continue. She also told him about her dreams and on the plane and she had picked up a copy of the book that he wrote. She also told him of the dream she had had before coming to the hospital. He asked her about the book and wanted to know why she brought a copy of it. She said that he wrote about the necklace in the book and some how is tied into what was going on.

"You where never the one to say what was exactly what you meant. I started to skim through the book while I was waiting for your family to leave and noticed that the book had many similarities with our own life together. The book is a bit more dramatic but there are still things that you really did not say. I want to know what the secret is." She said hoping that he would give her a clue.

"It is not for me to tell, it is true that some of the answers that you are looking for are contained within the book, and there are answers that you are going to have to figure out for yourself. I did not mean to do this but that was the only way you could try to think through any problem.

Thinking through a problem is always the best teacher. He also told her that he could not help this time even if I wanted too there were some serious things that they needed to talk about so the subject of the book would have to wait," Bryan was a bit more serious now.

She seemed to get mad because she hated it when he answered her questions with riddles or other questions. He saw the frustration in her face but when he mentioned talking with her about some serious things her face went pale as if what he was about to say was going to scare her. He said that there was nothing to be afraid of and that he was glad that she came but they needed to speak about some unfinished business.

Bryan looking more serious then ever now decided to talk first. "I have known that it has been a long time since we have talked, but this will be the last time I talk with you about such matters. Let's just drop all of the formalities and just be friends for the rest of the time and enjoy each other's company, okay?"

Misun agreed to his request.

"I want you to remember the Christmas a few years ago when we acted like—or should I say when we were *normal* people for a few days. I want us to talk like that now. So please hear me out," Bryan asked.

Again, Misun said, "Okay."

"I never wanted to interfere with your new life but I have to say that now you have a choice to make and there are no other options. If you love Rachel and Junior—as I know that you do—you are going to have to fight for them with all the powers that you have inside of your self. You are their mother and you have not shared in the responsibilities of raising them. My time is short and I can no longer take care of them. When I gave you, your freedom a few years ago I took on all the responsibilities for raising them and the only responsibility you had was that of your self. Now it is time to make a choice for their sake. It is your choice not anyone else's. If you made a decision right now it would not be the right one so I want you to sleep on it and give me your answer tomorrow," Bryan said.

Misun just nodded her head.

Bryan continued, "This was the worst thing that I had to say to you and I do feel better for having to say it. Now I should have said a few things a long time ago. I have kept few things to myself and I did not want to bother you with your new life. I wanted to say that I never stopped lov- ing you. I have loved you from the first time we meet so many years ago. I knew then that we shared intertwined lives. We neglected each other at times and forgot to listen to each other cries for the attention that we both needed. We started to our life together and eventually drifted apart never meeting each other half way. We stopped commu- nicating.

You sought attention elsewhere and I fell into taking care of the kids. We made it through many hard time but we did it together. We could never turn back the hands of time to try to make up for past mistakes or lost time. I have made many mistakes in my life and have paid for them in many different ways. Meeting you was never a mistake it was a blessing. You have made many mistakes as well. We could bicker about who did what first but in all of everything that has happened we had a chance to work this out but we both decided to keep it to ourselves and this is where we are today. I have thought about you many times and prayed for you, not in the sense that you would come back to me, but to pray that you where safe and that everything was okay. You have always brought out the best in me and I thank you for everything that you have done. I know that this may sound like a confession but that is what it is. Between us, there is nothing to forgive. Love understands and forgives all and there is a hidden power behind it that not many could ever understand. I have left you the house and everything there is yours for you have always been a part of it. The kids are in the guardianship of David and Anna. I know that you would have wanted it this way if something had happened to me. I have always needed you but never could bring myself to say it. I want to say more but my strength is going and I want to hear from you."

Misun looked up at Bryan quite saddened and began to speak in a low and soft voice, "Bryan, from what you have told me, I want to say that all you said was true and there was a time that we could have tried to work everything out and as you said we just couldn't say the words. I think back upon our life together and see many pictures of us. I see many happy times and many bad ones as well. I have always known how much you have loved me and the only thing that always kept me from coming back was my self-pride. I could never forgive myself for leaving you and the kids. I thought that when I met Kevin things would change and I would be able to forget about our life and the kids. I could never be loved by anyone in the way that you love the kids and me; this was a part of my world that I could never be able to forget. I would always think about you and the kids wondering what you are doing and how much they have grown. I tried to call so many times but always felt so ashamed of myself. I thought that I loved Kevin and he loved me in return. I found out later that his love was that of a possession. He wanted me to keep me from all of my friends and keep me caged up in a house. I could never go anywhere with out him. I guess the love that I had for him was out of the attention. He made me understand that I was only a possession. He was always very jealous of the mention of you and the kids. When I called, he would go to the store and buy something or go over to his friend's house and get drunk. Sometimes we would get into arguments over the phone calls. He once told me that I should have another child to get over missing Rachel and Junior I knew that I could never have a child for that reason. Rachel and Junior where born out of the love we had for each other this is what you have shown me as it turned out we were divorced a year later and went our separate ways. I came back to you and asked you for help once again. You have always helped me when I needed it. You have always given me what I needed and often given you have given more than you should have. I know that you have done without in order to help me. I thank you for all you have done for me. When I moved to Georgia to become a flight atten- dant, you where very supportive and gave me the money to get into the school. I know that this hurt you but that one time I wish that you could have asked me to come home. I wanted you to ask me. I would have stayed if you only had asked. I want you to tell me what your heart wanted and what I longed to hear so many times. You gave into me so many times when you should have just said what was on your mind. You always gave me my freedom and free reign to do what ever I wanted. You could never tell me no or explain what you felt. You made me so mad so many times because of this. I know that you never wanted to hurt my feelings but sometimes it is better to say something then nothing at all. I also hated the way you talked in riddles. If you would just say what you meant I could have figured out the rest. Now you are leaving me with one more riddle and that just irritates the hell out of me. I am sorry but you have to understand me. You know that I have a short temper and that I am impatient. So, Bryan, please no more rid- dles, okay? I have missed you and the kids every day. There is not a night that I sleep that I do not think about how you are doing. You have never asked for help from me, not once, not even when you left the Army and had a problem finding a job. How is it that you could not ask me? I would have helped you if only you would ask for it. I know that you could never ask for help from anyone unless it was so serious that you did not have a choice. You have lived your entire life alone and yet you were always content with every decision that you have ever made even if it was a bad one. I respect you for that because it has shown me how strong you are. Where most people would crumble you always found a way out of your situation and finished out ahead. You once told me that you were a great problem solver but you could not fix our problem. I admit that I did not help you very much. When we had a problem with finance, you fixed it. If there was a problem with the house, car or whatever you fixed all of them. I know that I should have told you what I needed from you but I thought that you would figure it out. You never did so I left. We should have talked about it but I was so lost and did not care about anything anymore my only option was to get out. I wish things where different and

I could go back but now it is really too late for that. We are talking as if we should have so many years ago, but now it is only to say good-bye for the last time. Right now, I feel so sorry for everything because it should not have to end like this. Bryan, as far as Rachel and Junior, I will do as you ask and think it tonight and I will let you know tomorrow. Bryan looked at Misun who was now crying. He reached out to her with his hand and grasping her hand pulled her close to him. She bent over to him, kissed him, and told him that she was so very sorry for everything. He looked up to her and told her that there was no need to feel sorry or pity now, now is the time we are sharing each other thoughts and it makes me happy to know that you still care.

She stood up and hit him softly in the arm and said, "You asshole." Bryan let out a phony cry and they laughed a little. "I am very glad that we have had this talk. It was long overdue. Too many years have gone bye and so much time was wasted. My love for you has never changed it only was silenced for a while." Bryan said.

Misun looked at Bryan smiling for the first time since she entered the room and said, "I am so happy to see you. You even as sick as you are can find humor where there is none. I always loved you for that. I know that it is getting late and you need to sleep. I will be going for now and I will be back tomorrow with my answer. I have always loved you but never knew how much until now."

Misun bent over to Bryan and kissed very passionately. Bryan did not object at all. After they kissed, Bryan looked up at her and told her that if they kissed any longer he would have to ask her to close the door and turn off the lights. Misun hit him in the arm again but this time Bryan did not say anything. They just looked at each other and smiled. She bent over, kissed him on his cheek, and whis- pered, "Good night my Bryan, I will see you tomorrow." Bryan reached over and spanked her on the butt and said, "Don't be a stranger." Misun grabbed his hand and held it for a few moments then let go of it, she turned and was heading for the door.

After Misun left, Bryan was so very happy. He was so glad that she came to see him. He so wished that they had this talk so many years ago. He always knew that she loved him but could never let himself stop her from leaving. He was feeling very exhausted now and had nothing left except to close his eyes and sleep. He thought to himself that tomorrow was a day that he did not want to come it he knew it would be his last. He thought, to night is not a night of dreams but a night of sleep. Slowly Bryan drifted of to sleep.

7

I walked out of Bryan's room and headed for the car. I felt so at peace with myself. We finally said the things we should have said to each other so many years ago. I knew that I had a decision to make, and I promised Bryan that I would sleep on it first. I needed to get something to eat. I only ate a cookie in the visitors' lounge waiting for his family to leave. I will probably have to eat at a fast food place it is getting late. I will take it back to my room and eat it there. I still need to read Bryans book. I am missing something. He wrote of many things, but there had to be a clue in his book. I needed to get back to my room so I can think this through.

Misun picked up something to eat on the way to her hotel, when she got to her room she felt very tired. She felt as if all the energy was draining from her. She did not know what was happening as felt very frightened. She opened the door to her room and went over to the bed. She sat down on the corner of her bed and tried to shake off this sense of energy drain. I was getting worse. She did not know how long she would be able to take this. She bent over and the necklace fell to the floor. Instantly she began to feel better. The glow from the necklace was gone. She reached for the necklace and as soon as she touched the necklace, she had another vision.

This vision was a very serious one. She was in Bryan's room. There were doctors and nurses standing all around him. There were many machines hooked up to Bryan, and at one point, she heard a doctor say, "We are losing him. Get the paddles!" Misun watched with intense horror. She did not know if this was really happening, or was it something that could happen. At one point, she saw the heart monitor flat line. The doctor grabbed the paddles and shocked him. They shocked him three times and the doctor screamed for adrenaline. A nurse gave him a long needle and the doctor stuck into his chest. The doctor waited for a few seconds. The doctor picked up the paddles again and shocked him once more. Slowly the heart monitor began to beat slow at first but steady. The beat got stronger as time continued. Misun was in pure shock. Then the vision faded.

Misun fell to the floor gasping for air. She thought dur- ing the whole vision that she was in so much shock she could not breathe. She laid there on the floor coughing and trying to breathe. After a few minutes, she was getting back to normal. She made her way to the bed and climbed onto it. She was still holding the necklace in her hand. She knew that she must have grabbed it during her vision. She looked at the necklace it was giving off a very dim glow. She calmed down enough to pick up the phone and called the hospital. After fifteen minutes of nurses, trying to locate someone to find out the status of Bryan a nurse asked her if she was family. Misun told her that she was his ex-wife and was there earlier to see him. Misun gave her name and the nurse looked up the name on the access roster. Bryan included her on this roster when they admitted him into the hospital. The nurse told Misun that twenty minutes ago Bryan went into cardiac arrest they had to move into intensive care for the rest of the night. He is doing well now; he could not have any visitors until his doctor checks on him in the morning. Misun thanked her and hung up the phone.

Misun began to cry. The vision that she just had was all- true. She had seen everything. She could do nothing but watch in horror. Misun could not hold back the sadness she had just felt and sobbed so hard that there was a knock on the door. She stopped crying just long enough to hear the knock on the door. A voice from outside the room asked if she was okay. She told the voice outside that she would be fine. She heard footsteps walking away. She lay back on the bed and looked across the room. Her food was on the table still in the bag. She could not bring herself to eating at this point. She got up, went over to the counter, and grabbed some tissue to wipe her eyes and blow her nose. She then looked into the mirror. She knew she looked terrible but this was something else. Her eyes were swollen and black from her mascara that ran from her eyes to her chin in many streaks. She looked very scary. She now remembered why Bryan called it war paint. She was truly scary enough. She half smiled and fixed herself up.

Misun now knew that she had to read more of Bryan's book. This was the only way even if she had to stay up all night to finish reading it. She looked at the small coffeepot on the counter and decided that it would be able to make four cups. "That would have to be enough," she said and made a cup of coffee.

Misun grabbed her coffee, walked over to the table, and grabbed her food. She knew that she was going to have to eat at some point, and even though her food was cold, it would be better than not eating at all. She walked over to the bed placed her coffee and food on the nightstand then propped up her pillows and sat down on the bed. When she was comfortable, she began to read.

As she read, she noticed that the events in the book were very similar to her life with Bryan. *Bill is the name of Bryan's character, and Laura is the name of mine.* Bryan did not get too much into detail, but the meaning was the same. This book brought back so many memories though some of them were very painful to want to remember. She kept reading wanting to find a clue to Bryan's sickness. There were times when she was laughing then crying and eventually had to place the book down because the memories hurt very deeply. She would get out of bed and have to go to the counter to grab some tissue to dry her eyes and blow her nose. She had no idea how hard it was to read his book.

She finally got to the part of the book where it talked about the necklace. She was wearing the very same one in every detail. It was now 3:00 a.m. She was getting tired, but she could not stop. She knew that she was getting close. She pressed on with the reading.

Misun read about Bill's hardships and felt so sorry for him. At one point, she thought that Bryan's sickness had derived from his loneliness and suffering but she knew that there must be more to it. Bill was stronger that that and she knew it. She came to the major difference between the book and her life now. In the book, a year and a half after Laura left Bill for the second time with her fiancé, she returned home once again. It was a stormy night and she was carrying a small bag in her arms. Bill let her in the house and made her comfortable. He went to get her a towel to dry off with and placed a pot on the stove to make something warm for her to drink. When he returned to the living room, she was holding a baby. The baby was around six months old. Bill loved children went over to her and looked at the baby. It was a baby boy with blue eyes and blond hair. Bill did not ask any questions, he just looked up at her and noticed that she was very sick. Bill asked her what was wrong and what could he do to help her. She smiled at him and told him that she would be fine after a shower and some sleep. She did not have to ask if Bill would take care of the baby. He would have insisted on it.

Laura drank some hot tea and talked with Bill for a wile. The baby was asleep. She got up from the couch and told Bill that she was going to take a shower and lie down on the couch if he did not mind. Bill told her that would be fine except that she could lie down on the bed in the bedroom and no one would disturb her while she slept. He told her that there were still some of her clothes hanging in the closet for her. He told her that he never moved them since she was here last. Bill told her not to worry about the baby he would watch over him until she was ready to take over. With nothing more to say, Laura went into the bedroom and looked in the closet. Nothing had changed he had left it just as if she was still living here. She noticed that he did wash them and hung them back up. Laura knew how much bill loved her and would always wait for her. Laura picked out a sleeping shirt. She smiled and remembered the day that bill gave it to her. It was on a Christmas about eight years ago. It was red with white stripes and had Minnie mouse on the front. She remembered that she told Bill that she would never wear it, which was never true she often wore it. She went into the bathroom and took a shower.

Laura can into the front room after her shower, still dry- ing her hair with a towel. Bill smiled and told her that she looked good wearing Minnie again. She just smiled and said you wish. Bill did not think anything of it but just smiled. They sat there for a few moments and Laura got up and walked over to Bill. Bill tried to get up but Laura's hand held him to his seat. Laura told him that it was not necessary for him to get up. She bent down to him and kissed him. She thanked him for helping her and that she needed to get some sleep. Bill told her to get some sleep and everything would be fine until morning. Laura was off to bed. She closed the door to the room behind her.

Bill would never interfere with her life and would not ask her questions that she did not want to answer so he just helped her with whatever she needed. He could not help to wonder why she looked so sick. He thought that maybe tomorrow she would tell him.

The next morning Bill woke up with the baby still in his arms. He remembered that during the night that he got up and feed the baby. He changed his diapers and rocked him back to sleep, just as he did with his children. He looked at the baby and noticed that the baby had a note next to his feet. Bill placed the baby on the couch. He was still asleep. Bill took the note and began to read:

Dearest Bill,

I am very sorry for having to do this, but you are the only one whom I could trust with my baby. I have to go away and do not know if I will be able to make it back in time. As you noticed, I am very sick and need treatment. I left for California to receive treat- ment for my sickness, so please take care of Patrick for me. You're a good father and a wonderful man, and Patrick is a good baby.

I know that you still love me, and I do still love you. But I must deal with this sickness first before we can think about anything else. I do love and miss the kids. Please tell them that for me. I did not want to do this, but there was no one else.

Love,
Laura

Bill was very hurt not that she left Patrick with him but the fact that she did not ask for his help. He would always help her when she asked. So why would she not ask this time, Bill wondered.

Bill new what he had to do. He called his friend and told her the story. She understood why she left the baby with

Bill but wondered what bill needed from her. Bill told her that he needed to find Laura and help her. He was going to have his family in California try to locate her by calling the hospitals in LA. Once he found her, he would need to fly there and make sure that she had everything that she needed and was getting the best of care. She knew what he wanted. He wanted her to watch over the kids when he left for California. She told him to let her know when he was leaving and she would be stay at his house until he returned. Bill thanked her and hung up the phone.

Bill now needed to try to find the father. He knew that his first name was John but that was it. He would have to make a few phone calls to some of their old friends to find out a last name with that he would try to locate the father. After calling several of their old friends, he got a last name it was Hutchings. Bills next call was to the police. He told them of what happened and wanted to know what he could do. They told him that a person from social services would be there later and that they would try to locate the father. They also asked him if they needed some one to come over and pick up the baby. He told them that he would take care of the baby and he would not be any problem.

The baby began to stir. Bill went over to the baby and attended to his needs. Bill would have to call his family later. While Bill was tending to the baby, his own children woke up and went into the living room. They saw their father holding a baby. They were very surprised to see this. The walked over to him and asked him where did the baby come from. Bill looked over at the kids and told them what happened last night. The kids were still confused about all of this. They walked toward the baby and took a closer peak at the baby. Junior did know what to think but April smiled and said that he was so cute. Bill told them that he thought that this baby was their half brother. April was happy to have another little brother while Junior just said great I have a baby brother. April told Junior that she did not have to call him little brother anymore because they had a new baby brother. Junior smiled and said, "That's okay with me,

I am no longer the little brother." They asked his name and both of them started to play with the baby.

A woman from social services arrived at Bill house a couple hours after Bills call. She knocked on the door and asked to go in. Bill let her in and they both sat down and talked. Bill wanted to foster the child until they could locate his father. The woman said that there would be paperwork to fill out and that she did not see any problems. In a way, the child is a relative to his children. She had some papers that he had to fill out she told him that he would have to go to her office later and fill out some more paper work. She did not for see any problems with leaving the child in Bill's care.

After the woman from social services left, Bill called his family in California. He talked with his mother and his brother. He did eventually convince them into helping him even though they did not like this scenario.

A week went bye before Bill received any news. The police called to inform him that the baby's father has not been located yet we are still looking. They would keep trying. Bill thanked the officer. He asked him to keep him informed if anything else came up. The officer said no problem and hung up the phone.

It was an hour latter that Bill received a call from his brother in California. He told bill that they think they found Laura. She was staying a cancer treatment center in LA and from what they told; him was that she was in real bad shape. Bill told his brother that he would be there in the morning. Bill thanked his brother and hung up the phone. It was late afternoon; Bill called his friend and arranged for her to watch the kids for a couple of days. He told the kids that he needed to go somewhere and that he would be back in a day or two. He told them that their favorite friend was coming over to stay with them. They where sad to see their father go but they go used to him leaving from time to time. He often had to leave to sign books. He was a writer too. Sometimes he would take them with him but this time they could not go. The kids loved their sitter she was like their Nanny her name was Nancy. Nancy filled in for bill while he was away. She would take them for walks and the park, if they where good, she would take them for ice cream. Bill and Nancy had been good friends for the last four years. Bill never knew that Nancy really liked him. Nancy was thirty-five years old and was very pretty. Bill told the kids that the Patrick had to go with him. It was important that he went. The kids were did not want him to go. They liked having a little brother around.

Bill called the airport and arranged to fly to California the next morning. He called Nancy and told her what time he needed her to come over. She told him that she would be there. Bill was ready except for packing some clothes and a bag for the baby. Bill had a hard time getting used to hav- ing a baby in the house. He was glad that he did not have nine-to-five job. He now had a routine and it worked out well for the baby and the kids. Bill packed the bags and set them by the front door for tomorrow morning.

They all ate dinner that Bill cooked and the Bill fed the baby while trying to eat his own meal. After dinner, the kids rinsed off the plates and placed them into the dishwasher. They all moved into the living room to watch TV. It was time for the kids to get ready for bed. The baby had fallen asleep shortly before. The kids got up front the couch and headed into the bathroom to brush their teeth and wash their faces. Bill followed behind them. Bill tucked each one into their beds and kissed them good night.

Bill walked into the living room and turned of the TV and the lights. It was now time for him to go to sleep too. He had a busy day tomorrow and would need the sleep.

Bill was up early the next morning, and to his surprise, the kids were up as well. Bill was glad that the baby only woke him up once during the night. Bill made every- one something to eat and went to take a shower and get dressed. He was walking out of his room, still buttoning his shirt on, when he noticed that Nancy was already there. They greeted each other and went through the formalities of phone numbers and times for everyone.

Nancy said, "Everything's going to be okay. Not to worry. Take care and be careful." Bill told the kids it was time for him to go now. The kids ran over to him and hugged and kissed him. They said good-bye and went back to watching TV. Bill went to Patrick, who was asleep, and placed him into his basket. He asked Nancy if she would help him with the bags to the car. Nancy was happy to help. They walked out to the car and bill place the baby in his car seat while Nancy placed the bags into the trunk.

Bill walked over to Nancy, hugged her, and told her that he would be back soon. She told him that she would be right here if he needed her. They just smiled at each other, and Bill got into the car and was off to the airport.

Bill made to the airport, checked his bags in, and headed for his gate. He was on the plane and heading for California.

Once in California, Bill picked up his rental car and drove to his mother's house. He stayed there for a little while talking with everyone. His brother finally arrived and spoke with bill. He gave Bill all of the information that he needed to see Laura. He asked his mother if she could watch the baby for him while he went to the hospital. He wanted to take the baby but he did not know if they would let him in to see her if, he had Patrick. She said it would be fine. Bill kissed her and was off to the hospital.

Bill arrived at the hospital at 3:15 p.m. He went to the counter and asked to see Laura Hutchings. The woman at the counter asked his drivers license. Bill handed to her and she checked his name with the access rooster. She handed bill back to him and told him that her room was down the hall to the right in room 112. Bill thanked her and headed for Laura's room.

Bill entered her room. He thought she was sleeping. He moved closer and she opened her eyes. "I hope that you didn't think you could run out on me did you?" Bill said with a smile.

"I didn't want you to see me like this. I was hoping that I would get better first before I went back to see you. I am sorry but I do not think that will happen now. The doctor told me that the cancer has spread through out my body and it is too late to try anything. I do not have much time." Laura said through her tears. She was crying.

Bill went over to her and grabbed her hand. Bill was at a loss for words. He did not know what to say. Bill held her and let her cry. She cried for a few minutes. Bill had tears running from his eyes as well.

Laura stopped crying and lay back on the bed. She looked at Bill and told Bill that she has something for him. She reached into a drawer and pulled out a small box. She handed it out Bill and told him that she could no longer wear it and that it had to back to you. Bill opened the box and pulled out the necklace. Laura grabbed the necklace and held it out for Bill to place his head through the loop. Bill did not object to wearing the necklace. Once the neck- lace was on bill it began to glow but only for a few seconds then it went out.

"That's it. I have to give Bryan the necklace back. I cannot believe it was that simple. I know what to do," shouted Misun in excitement.

She looked over at the clock on the table. It read now 6:21 a.m.

She decided to take a nap before she would head for the hospital. It has been a long night for her and she was feeling very happy knowing that he knew what to do. She rolled on her side and fell asleep.

8

Bryan open his eyes, the world seemed to be out of focus. He opened and closed his eyes several time before they began to focus. He felt very stiff and sore. He turned his head and noticed that he was no longer in his room. He saw that he had IV's stuck in each arm. He did not know what was going on. He reached for the button to call a nurse but one had just walked in. He asked the nurse why he was in this room and not his own. She told him that his doctor would arrive soon and would explain everything to him when he arrived. Bryan was very confused and wondered why she would not tell him.

The nurse took his blood pressure and temperature picked up his chart and recorded her reading. Bryan asked her how long will it be before the doctor is here. The Nurse said that he should be here in the next thirty minutes. Bryan asked her what time it was. She told him that it was now 10:00 a.m. "Is there anything that I could get for you?" she asked. He asked her for a cigarette. She just shook her head and walked out of the room.

Bryan did not like this nurse too much. He looked around the room and noticed that it looked more like an ICU ward. He now knew where he was. He wondered why he was here. All he could remember was falling asleep last night. He would have to wait until the doctor showed up before he would find out the answers.

The doctor walked into the room. He was carrying Bryan's chart in his hand. Bryan tried to ask a question; but the doctor merely said, "One moment and I would be right there to answer your questions." After looking through Bryan's chart, the doctor walked over to him and looked at his eyes, felt his neck, and listened to his heartbeat. The doctor told Bryan that he gave the staff quite a scare last night. Bryan asked the doctor what he meant by that all he could remember was falling asleep. The doctor said if his staff did not react as quickly as they did it might have been a permanent one. Bryan was astounded to hear this news. He told the doctor that he felt fine this morning and wanted to know when he will be able to move back into his room. The doctor told Bryan that if his vitals stay constant for the next few hours that he will move him back into his room but the heart monitor and IVs will stay on. Bryan agreed. Bryan told the doctor that he has family coming this afternoon and that he needed to see them it was very important for him. The doctor looked at Bryan and told him that he will move him back to his room by lunchtime. After the Doctor left,

Bryan called for the nurse. He asked the nurse if he could get something to eat. The nurse told him that breakfast had already passed. Bryan was very hungry for the first time in weeks. He asked the nurse if they had a cafeteria some where in the hospital. She told Bryan that they had a very nice one in the basement. He asked her if there was any way that she or someone she knew could get him a nice juicy cheeseburger with some fries. She told him that there might be such a person but it will cost you a side of fries. Done, Bryan said, He asked her if she found his pants there was money in his wallet. She told Bryan that he could pay her back later. She smiled and walked out of the room. Bryan could not believe how hungry he was. His stomach was making funny noises. It was twenty minutes before someone entered the room. It looked like he was an orderly. Bryan could tell that by the way he was dressed. He said to Bryan "room service." He told Bryan that if he was caught doing this he would get into a lot of trouble. Bryan told him that he would not tell a soul. The orderly sat a bag on the counter next to the bed and said good-bye to Bryan.

Bryan opened the bag. Inside the bag was a white box. He took the box out of the bag and placed it in front of him. He opened the box and looked inside. There was a large cheeseburger and fries. He looked in the bag to see if there were any ketchup packets in it. (He did not like to eat fries without ketchup.) There were only three packets.

This would have to do. He poured ketchup over his fries and picked up his cheeseburger. It was hot and dripping. He took one bite of the burger. To his delight, it was the best burger that Bryan had ever eaten. He finished about half of the burger and some of the fries when the doctor walked in. The doctor looked at Bryan and asked just took another bite of the burger. "Where did you get that food?" the doctor said with a stern voice.

Bryan finished chewing and looked at the doctor. He knew that he was in trouble. All he could do was offer a bite to the doctor. The doctor just looked at Bryan and shook his head.

"I guess that you are feeling better, and you are trying to get some of my staff in trouble. I know that you put some-one up to this, so let's just get rid of the food and get you back up to your room. I can't have anyone eating in the ICU ward. It is against policy," the doctor said with a smile and walked out of the room.

Bryan could not wait to get back to his room. He knew that his family would be here very soon. He did not want to loose the burger and fries but he knew that it was for the better. He hoped that no one was in trouble.

A nurse entered the room and took the food from Bryan. Bryan was scrambling to try to finish what ever he could before the nurse took it from him. He told the nurse that he hooped that he did not get her into too much trouble.

She told him that all the doctor said was that he hoped that this would never happen again.

She took the food and placed it into the bag. She told Bryan that the orderly would be in here in a few minutes to move him back into his room. She told him that the rest of his food would be waiting when he arrived. Bryan was happy.

A few minutes later, an orderly and another nurse walked into the room. They took off all of the monitors but left one IV in his arm. They brought in a wheelchair and seated Bryan onto it. Soon, they were on their way to Bryan's room.

Bryan was so happy to be back into his room. The nurs- ing staff had been very kind to Bryan. The orderly helped Bryan get back into his bed. He asked the orderly to get his wallet that was in his pants hanging up in the closet. The orderly did as he asked. Bryan took out two twenty-dol- lar bills and gave them to the orderly. He told the orderly one was for him for getting his food for him and the other was for the nurse. Bryan told him not to worry about the change and it was well worth it. The orderly thanked Bryan and told him that if he every needed his services again to just have the nurse send for him. Bryan tanked him and the orderly left the room.

Bryan sat back on his bed, reached over to the table, and grabbed the bag that was on it. He finished his food even though it was a little cold by now. He still enjoyed every bite.

It was now nearing 1:00 p.m., Bryan sat back on his bed and thought about Rachel and Junior He remembered the day that they were born.

It was late January when Misun and I arrived in California. I left the army to begin a new life for Misun and me. She did object to me leaving but I assured her that everything was going to be fine. I would be living at my parent's house until I got a good job to support us. Misun and I save up some money to get started with our new life.

I was doing some house remolding jobs for a short time to keep an income for us. It did not pay a lot. Daren, my brother-in-law was looking for a job at his work for me. He was a good man. Daren was my best friend before I introduced him to my sister Casey.

Misun was having a hard time trying to adjust to a new culture and my family. She wanted to go home at one point and I talked her out of it. I knew that she was sacred. She became ill one night and I had to take her to the hospital. They took some blood and ran some tests. They said that she would be fine once she started to take some medication for her infection. I was glad that it was not too serious but she was in pain.

A week later, she was sick again. I took her back to the hospital once again. She had another problem and it was not serious. They prescribed some medication and we went home. I did not know what was going on. The trips to the hospital were very expensive and it was draining away our savings. I was glad hat I started to work with Daren the week before. I would not have insurance for another eleven weeks.

A few days later Misun was not feeling well. I looked at her and asked her if she was pregnant. She looked at me and said she did not think so. We went to the drug store and bought a couple of those pregnancy tests that sold over the counter. We went straight home.

Misun went into the bathroom and used the first one. She called me into the bathroom and showed me the results. The test was positive. Misun wanted to try another one. I let her use all three and they all came back positive. She wanted to be sure. I took Misun to the hospital the next morning and they ran a pregnancy test on her. It too came back positive. I was very happy. I was going to be a father. I could not wait to tell my family.

During Misuns pregnancy, I had a dream of a little girl. I so wanted to have a girl. Every time that we went for her checkup and used the sonogram the baby was facing the wrong way. Misun wanted to now. I already knew from my dream.

It was the middle of November, when Misun and I were blessed with an eight pound ten ounce baby girl. I was in the delivery room the whole time. I was so happy I almost fainted. We had forgot to cut Misun's nails before we went to the hospital and by the time the baby was delivered my arms were bleeding and cut pretty good. The doctor tended to Misun while a nurse tended to my arms. I held her in my arms for the first time. I was in heaven. I started to cry. I just could not believe that this child was ours. I walked over to Misun, holding the baby and put the baby into Misun's arms. Misun began to cry. It was the happiest day of my life. The nurse asked Misun and me what her name was going to be. Misun and I never gave it much thought. I looked at Misun and asked her what she thought about Rachel. Misun like the sound of it and that became her name.

Misun and I were very happy parents. It was hard at first but once the baby established a routine, we were able to sleep more than a couple of hours here and there. I got up most of the nights to feed her and change her diapers. Misun would wake many times just to find me sitting on the couch asleep with Rachel still in my arms.

My work was downsizing due to the military cuts. My work did a lot for the military and when the Military cancelled a lot of it contracts, we lost a lot of work. I had been working for them for two years now. Rachel was two now. I lost my job since I was the last machinist hired. I knew it was going to happen. I looked for work and there were no jobs openings.

Misun and I sat down at the table in our apartment and talked about me going back into the Army. I needed to take care of my family. We agreed that I would go back into the Army. I knew that I would loose a pay grade for being out over two years but it was what I had to do. We decided that she and Rachel would go to Korea and stay with her family while I got back into shape and went through the paper- work trail of enlisting back into the army.

Misun was excited to go back to Korea to see her family. She so wanted to show Rachel to all of them. I was happy for them. I was going to stay with Casey and Daren while I waited on the paperwork for enlisting.

It took a couple of weeks to get Rachel passport. A day or two later, I took Misun and Rachel to the airport. I kissed both of them good-bye and put them on a plane heading for Korea. I cried one the way home. I was alone.

I moved in with Casey and Daren a few days later. The enlistment officer said that I would have to go Airborne if I wanted to back into the Army. I thought that was cool. I wanted to go airborne the first time but it was not an option then. He said that I should be back in the Army within a month. I rally did not want to wait that long but that was fine with me. It was going to give me more time to get back into shape.

Three weeks later, I was on a plane heading for Ft. Benning, Georgia. I had to get through airborne school before I would have and assignment. I finished airborne school and was back on a buss headed for Fort Bragg, North Carolina, home of the 82nd infantry.

I settled into my job and looked forward to seeing Misun and Rachel. I called them every chance that I had. I had to wait on paperwork to be able to send for them. The paperwork took a few weeks and I sent for them.

I picked them up at the airport and was so very happy. I felt that my life was whole once again. I was not alone anymore. We drove back to Fayetteville and stayed at the Army's courtesy housing until we found an apartment. We found and apartment the next week.

I bought a new car before they arrived and it was perfect for the three of us. We moved into our apartment and it was fun helping decorating it with Misun and Rachel. We were a family once again. It was nice.

Misun loved Fayetteville because of all of the oriental markets. Fayetteville had many soldiers that were married to Korean women; it would not be hard for Misun to find some new friends.

We all settled in our new life for a few months when Misun became sick. It seemed to be the same routine as with Rachel so we had a pregnancy test done. It came back positive. I was going to be a father once again. I was very happy. Misun could not believe it. She was not ready for another child. I cold see it in her eyes. I told her that everything was going to be fine. She looked at me and made me promise.

Money was better once I received a promotion. I was back to the same rank before I left the Army. I spent a lot of time in the field and was worried because the baby was due just before I was going on a deployed for a month. Misun had found some good friends and was not worried anymore. Rachel was excited that she was going to have a baby sister or brother. She wanted a sister. I told her that it was going to be a little brother. She asked me how I knew. I told her of the dream I had one night a few months ago. I was holding hands with a little girl and a little boy that is how I knew. I told Misun this same story a few months ago and she said no way. She told me that everyone she knew even her mother said it was a girl. We had many sonograms done and. The baby had turned in the wrong direction to be able to tell.

It was March when the baby arrived. I was at the hospital with Misun. This time we did cut her nail before we went to the hospital. The doctor asked me what did I want a boy or girl. I told the doctor that I wanted to see my son. The doctor asked if I knew from the sonogram. I said no I just knew. Misun gave birth to a baby boy. He was eight pounds, fourteen ounces, and twenty-three inches long. He was a big boy. The doctor let me cut the umbilical cord. I was so nervous I almost dropped the scissors.

They cleaned up the baby and handed him to me. A nurse grabbed my arm. I almost fainted. To see my son for the first time there was no feeling that would ever come close to this. I walked over to Misun and put him in her arms. She looked at him and smiled. I looked back at her a bent over to kiss her and thank her for being a beautiful mother and a loving wife.

Misun and the baby, we named Bryan William McIntire III, came home three days later. We let Rachel hold her new brother with our supervision. She was just amazed. She starred at him for a few minutes then began to talk to him. All Misun and I could do was watch her.

· · · · · · · · · ● · · · · · · · · · ·

Over the next year and a half, Misun and I were amazed at everything happening in our lives. Rachel loved her little brother. She was always protective of him. Rachel really wanted Little Bryan to grow so that they could play together.

Little Bryan was about a year and a half old when he talked to me and Misun. We were watching TV. He looked at us very seriously. He said that he no longer wanted to be called little Bryan, that he wanted to be called Junior. I looked at Misun and asked her what she thought about this. She just looked at me and shrugged. I asked Bryan why he wanted to be called Junior. He just said that he liked it better. Since then, he was called Junior.

Everything was going well for our family. There was one thing that we needed to do: Misun and I decided to buy a house for our family. We thought that apartment living was not the way to raise our children. We wanted a house with a backyard and (a fence so that they could play by them- selves) and a school close by.

We found a house that was perfect for all of us. I had only two requirements for a house: it had to have a two-car garage and a fireplace. The rest was up to Misun. Anyway, we hit the jackpot with the house we picked out: it was new, met my requirements, and had three bedrooms and a backyard. I built a fence around the backyard for the kids. We pretty much had everything now. Life was good.

Four months later, I received orders for Korea. I had to report there in two months. I was adding a screened-in patio to the back of the house that time, and afterward, I just hoped to have it done before I left. It was a non– command-sponsored tour. I was not able to take my fam- ily with me. I was going to have to say good-bye to them once again.

I finished the patio at 10:00 p.m. the night before I had to leave. My neighbors helped me with the roof. I said good-bye to them and went into the house to be with my family. I walked in the door, cleaned myself up, sat with my kids, and watched TV with them. This was my last night with my family.

A little while later, it was time for them to go to bed. I had a shuttle bus picking me up in the morning to take me to the airport. I did not want to drag the kids out of bed so early. So I picked them up and carried them off to bed. (They slept in the same room for now.) I kissed and hugged each one before walking out.

I walked into the living room, where Misun was still sit- ting on the couch. I asked her if she would like to go to bed now. She reached for my hand. I took hers in mine, and we both walked into our bedroom together. It was going to be the last night we shared together for a while.

When I woke up the next morning, I took a quick shower. I was dressed and walked out into the living room. Misun was already up and made me a cup of coffee. We drank our morning brew together.

Shortly thereafter, I heard the shuttle pulled up into the driveway and honked its horn. I kissed Misun, slipped into the kids' room, and kissed them on the forehead before I left.

These were my last good memories before everything changed. I decide to sleep before everyone showed up. A small tear ran down my face. Then I closed my eyes.

9

Misun woke up with many different thoughts in her head. She knew the necklace would help Bryan did not understand how. Bryan loved riddles. She knew there was something else that Bryan did not say in the book. It was now 2:30 p.m. She had to get up and get ready to go to the hospital.

Misun got up from her bed and walked over to take a shower. She stripped off all of her clothes and jumped into the shower. She still was puzzled over the book and the necklace. She finished taking her shower and dried off then got dressed. She was still not completely sure what she had to do.

She decided to finish Bryan's book. She thought their must be another clue. She went back to her bed and picked up the book. She began to read the final chapter.

As she read the final pages, she could not help for feeling sorry for Bill and Laura. Bill's pain for her loss made her cry. It was heartbreaking to continue to read of his life after Laura died. She never knew that love could mean every thing to someone.

As she read further, she came across a part of the book that almost looked as though it was missing a few page. She read about Bill returning home and telling his chil- dren about the death of their mother. Bill found out where Patrick's father was and that he wanted noting to do with the boy. Bill talked to the social worker and worked out adopting Patrick. Bill had to pay Patrick's father a lot of money to sign over custody of Patrick. Bill later dismantled the ring and gave the chains to his daughter. The crystal and ruby went to his son. Bill kept the ring and continued wear it just as before. It was the token of her love for him. He would take the ring off from time to time and read the inscription on the inside. There were just three little initials. FLB. This meant "Forever Love, Bill." Bill wrote a poem to remember his love.

> You take my hand, and you touch my heart
> I gave you a rose because you gave me need
> You gave me your love, and you gave me life

The poem was very simple, but it had so much meaning. Misun remembered when Bryan would write to her. Sometimes he would write little poems. Most of them were silly. The chapter skipped from this passage to were

Bill raised the children together. He wrote more books and never married again. The children grew up and went to college. In Bill later years he often passed the cemetery where he had a plaque made for Laura. Laura's body was sent home to Korea to be buried in the family plot. He knew that she would have wanted it this way. So bill had a plaque placed on an empty grave in remembrance of her. It was a place that he would go and talk to her and remember.

Bill died later of old age. He was eighty-four years old. His children, now adults, had his ashes buried in Laura's grave. They knew how much their father loved her, and it was right to have his last request granted.

There was a large funeral. So many people came to see him to say good-bye. Everyone who read Bill's books loved them. When his ashes were laid to rest in Laura's grave, his children were the only ones present. It was what he wanted. The inscription on his plaque read, "Devoted father and loving husband. Finally, he and his beloved Laura are together for eternity."

Misun cried for some time. She had no idea that his book was so beautiful and yet so sad. She knew now why the book sold many copies. She put the book down and looked at the necklace. She wondered if there was an inscription on it as well. It would have to be very small, and she never even thought about looking before. But when she did, there it was. She was able to make out three letters: FLB. They were the same three letters as in the book. "Forever Love, Bryan. That's what they mean!" Misun said, a little excited.

She looked over to the clock on the table. It was now 4:00 p.m. She really had no time now. *I have to hurry to the hospital!* Misun grabbed her purse and keys and headed out the door. She got into the car and sped off as she headed for the hospital.

While she was driving off to the hospital to see Bryan, she thought about what she had to do. She knew that she had to give the necklace back to him. Something was still niggling in the back of her mind, but she did not know what it was.

She was almost at the hospital when it came to her. She stopped the car in the middle of the road. Car horns blared, and a few people yelled curses at her. Now she knew what she had to do, so she rolled down her window and yelled out an apology before driving off. She had to make one last stop before visiting Bryan at the hospital. She hoped that there was going to be enough time because the neck- lace began to pulse. This stop had to be made; it was very important to her and Bryan.

She held the necklace and said, "Please, Bryan, hang on just a little bit longer. I know what to do now, so please stay with me."

10

The time was now 6:15 p.m. I know that I had only but a few minutes left until it was all over. I kissed the kids on the head and told them that I loved them for the last time. They looked up at me and they knew that I was going away. They just held onto me as if trying to keep me from leaving. They did not know that there was nothing that they could have that prevent me from leaving. I smiled at them and just enjoyed holding them close.

I looked around the room and saw many sad and long faces. They too where trying to hold back the tears. I could only smile and speak only my last words to them. I said, "I love you and I will miss all of you." They all could not hold their tears any longer. They began to cry.

I looked toward the window and peered out catching the last rays of the sun. I prayed to God for the life that I had lived and thanked him for all of the love and compas- sion that he has always shown to me over the years. I asked him to forgive my family and help them throughout the rest of their lives and asked him to watch over my children.

For the first time I felt as if, he was listening to me. His presence was very near.

I felt my heart slowing down and suddenly I felt very tired. It was time for me to go. I had wished that the love of my life were here so that I could find out what her decision was. I will try to hold out for as long as I can but it would only be minutes.

Misun entered the room and looked over toward the bed. In that instant, she knew that there was no time to spare. She hurried over to the bed and placed her hand on my face. She looked at me with more care and compassion that I had ever seen in her eyes. She asks the kids to move off the bed so that she could speak with me and that she would speak with them after she took care of their dad. The kids nodded their head and moved off the bed but stayed very close. She sat down on the bed very near me. I tried to say something but she placed her finger over my lips and told me that I had done enough talking for now so listen to what she had to say, so conserve your strength and listen. I nodded my head.

Misun began to speak.

"First, I want to tell you how wonderful you are. I know that you have sacrificed your life so that I would be able to have my own life. I also know that you where always with me because the necklace that you gave me was more than just a necklace. You had sealed part of your soul in it to protect me and watch over me. Therefore, I have something that I want to give to you. I love you Bryan. I have always loved you. I abused your love for me only because I did not understand it. I never understood the true meaning of love until now. I hope that you can forgive me."

She took the necklace off from around her neck and placed it over Bryan's heart. The necklace began to glow once again.

Bryan said for the last time, "Honey, there is nothing to forgive. But I ask you now…what is your decision?"

Before she could reply, there was another flash of light, and Bryan was gone, his eyes closed. Misun began to cry. The whole room knew what had just happened. There was not a dry eye left in the room. Rachel and Junior held each other and began to cry.

Misun reached into her jacket pocket and pulled out a small wedding band. She placed it on Bryan's finger. Then she kissed Bryan and said, "I wish you could hear me. I chose you, my husband. I will always love and miss you."

A single tear ran down her face and dripped onto the necklace. A warm white glow emanated from the necklace. It started to expand with every passing second until the light filled the room. No one knew what was happening; all they could do was watch.

Bryan, Misun, and the children were surrounded by this strange light, which, seemingly, nothing could penetrate. They were completely absorbed by the light, hidden from the rest of the people in the room. To top that off, not even a sound could be heard from the light. All the spectators could do was watch and wait.

The light gave off a warm glow. Misun and the kids were very startled and did not understand what was happening. Suddenly, a voice came from the light and spoke.

"It is true that you saved his soul, but it was not enough to save his life. He had sacrificed everything for love, and what concerns me is the way that he did this. It is very rare in this age that someone would take such risks and be so reckless to go to such extremes for love. He has shown me that love does still exist in this—in *your* world.

"Your world is full of people who are indifferent to eve- rything around them. They run back and forth, not car- ing about anyone but themselves. There are not very many people who will pass the plate—many would rather pass the *buck*. When most people tell someone that they love them, they mean that they love them until something better comes around. The true meaning of love has been lost over time.

"People are more interested in getting what they can now without having to understand it or work for it. Even if they have to lie, cheat, or steal it from someone else. Love has become a convenience—nothing more. It is easier to love money and material things, like, cars, houses, and items that to some have sentimental worth, than to share their lives with someone else. This world has become lost to the value of the dollar than to the value of life.

"The ability to create life and watch it grow and flourish is one of the most precious gifts a person could ever have. Love is handed down from your mother and father,

experienced by all as they grow up in life. If one has never seen or felt what love is, they will never be able to pass this knowledge on through to their children. This is a common dilemma in your modern society.

"Many say that I have turned my back on your world. That statement is almost true. I cannot but feel pity that so many have lost their way. I have given your world everything. They have become very greedy and have taken everything but still want more.

"Man has grown insensitive to the needs of others. There will never be an end until humankind brings it upon him. Man will destroy man until nothing is left. The end of humankind will come when there is no longer any love for one another left in the world. Without love, no one man, women child or animal will survive its destruction. Man has corrupted themselves with greed, lust and power. This evil is of human making no ones else's.

"I no longer understand your world and leave it to its end but when someone risks everything not for power, or greed but for love, I must focus my attention to it. This man was full of life and loved everything around him. He showed his children that even a flower has more beauty than a piece of gold. He showed them how to love animals and care for the environment. He told them they have as much right to live as they do. He showed them how to care for and nurture these pets. He has given the building blocks of love. Your children will grow and become loved by all.

He alone has changed the fate of many. His place in heaven was secured until he decided one day to throw everything away. All he wanted was to show that love has no bounds and a life could be sacrificed to save another. A simple act that in itself was very selfish it could never go unnoticed. His love was unconditional to be true but the act of giving up his soul to care for someone that he could have never seen again was remarkable. A person can live without love but they cannot live without a soul not for very long any- way. From the moment he gave you the necklace he began to die. His life would eventually fade away. In his mind, he hoped and prayed that you would return but it did not mat- ter to him as long as you were safe.

"He is with me now because you gave back his soul. As for you, you could have chosen a different path; you chose to understand this love and had hoped that your actions would have saved him. In many ways, you did save him for without doing what you have done his soul would have never reached me. His soul would have stayed sealed in the necklace for eternity. You chose to love him and gave your life back to him by presenting a token of love once again. I am deeply pleased. Such devotion and faith for love cannot go without notice. I will grant you one request. You may have any wish that you want within reason. I do not usually come down to earth to interfere with anyone's affairs. I have watched this story unfold and with great concern and admiration…So what is your wish?"

Misun was still in shock about all of this. She looked down to Bryan and spoke to the voice, "I wish to be with my husband. That is my wish."

"Your husband is with me. Do you wish to come with me as well? If you come with me, you will die on earth as well. Think well my dear child for there are others on earth that will need you," the voice replied.

"I found out what life was all about through his love and his sacrifices. To leave him now would not be just. As he was willing to die for me, I am willing to die for him. That is my decision and my wish," Misun said with all con- fidence in the world.

Everyone in the room noticed that the light was fading and were able to hear Misuns last words.

"I will grant you your wish but not as you think. I will give Bryan's life back to you, so that your teaching of love may flourish in your children. Love gives us hope and hope gives us meaning to live. With this knowledge there still is hope for mankind if we just sit down and listen to each other and learn that life is a gift not something to be trifled with. Everyone has needs but if we communicate those needs, so that they are known and understood. No one is a mind reader. Appreciate everything around you; a flower or a fish swimming in a stream. Life has many beautiful wonders if we just open or eyes to the world around us. It is hard to live if we go through life wearing blinders impervi- ous to the world. Care for your family and others around you. Help those who are in need. Care not for payment from those you've helped. Your kindness will always come back to you. You are all my children and I do love you. Now go in peace." The voice said fading away.

No one in the room could move. They were still in shock for what had just happened. They all looked over to Bryan. Misun looked down at Bryan. She began to smile and reached out to touch his face. She said to him that it was now time to wake. Bryan began to breath and opened his eyes to see Misun smiling at him. He did not say anything. He reached up to her and pulled her down to him. They kissed with more passion then ever before. After they had kissed, Misun told Bryan that he would need to rest and build up his strength. She told him that she would never leave his side ever again. She said that she would take care of the children until he was well enough to go home and that they would all go home together.

Misun told the children to give their dad a kiss and hug. She told the children that she was going to take them home and that they would be back to see him tomorrow. The children did as she asked and climbed off the bed and grabbed Misuns hand. Misun walked over to where the others were standing. She asked the others if it was all right to take the kids with her for the night. No one objected to her request. They all knew what just happened and were now happy that she had come. Misun looked back over to Bryan and blew him a kiss. Bryan blew her a kiss back. Misun walked out of the room and down the hall with Rachel and Junior.

Bryan's family walked over to him and began to cry. Bryan looked at his family and told them that he was going to be fine now. He thanked all of them for coming to see him and that they need to stay for a little while longer if they could because there was gong to be a wedding and everyone was invited. Bryan's father told him that he would not miss it for anything. Bryan's sisters and Mother started to talk about thing that they could do for the wedding. Bryan just shook his head.

Bryan family did not stay at the hospital very long after Misun left. They knew Bryan needed to rest. This has been a day to remember for them. They all kissed Bryan welcomed him back.

It took a few weeks for Bryan to get back to almost full strength. Misun and the kids went and visited him every day. His family went back home until the wedding day which was the day after Bryan was released from the Hospital.

The wedding ceremony was on a beach. Everyone was there. Bryan paid for his family to be there and his publishers paid for the wedding. It was a beautiful wedding. There was not a dry eye in the crowd. Misun wore a beautiful white dress, the very same dress she wore in the pictures that they had taken in Korea before Bryan left. Bryan wore the same gray tuxedo as well. They never had a real wedding when they were first married, so it was only fitting that they would dress like they did in the pictures.

After the wedding ceremony and the reception party that lasted for many hours, Bryan and Misun had the kids spend a couple of days with his family while they headed home. Bryan drove up to the house and parked the car. He got out of the car and walked over to Misun's side. Then he opened her door, and she got out.

They walked over to the front door, and Bryan unlocked it. Bryan picked her up in his arms, kicked open the door, and carried her over the threshold. Once they were inside the house, she slid down so that she could stand on her feet next to Bryan.

He looked at her and said, "Welcome home."

She looked at him and said, "I am glad to be home." They kissed and Bryan kneed the door closed.

Just then, a giggle came from behind the door, and a voice said something like, "I know that it has been a while, but I am sure that I will be up to the task."

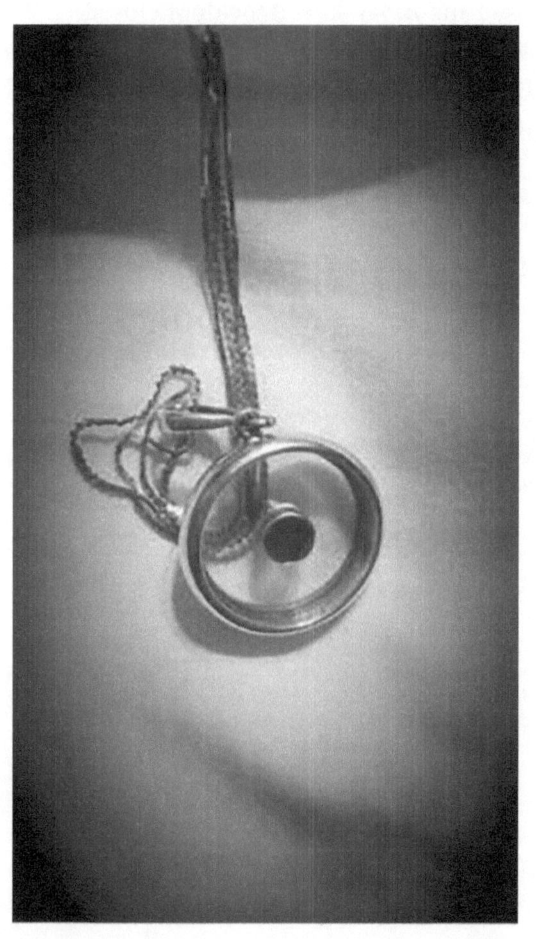

www.ingramcontent.com/pod-product-compliance
Lightning Source LLC
Chambersburg PA
CBHW030901200726
48289CB00003B/842